INVISIBLE THINGS

ALSO BY JENNY DAVIDSON

The Explosionist

INVISIBLE THINGS

Jenny Davidson

HARPER TEEN
An Imprint of HarperCollins*Publishers*

HarperTeen is an imprint of HarperCollins Publishers.

Invisible Things

 For information address HarperCollins Children's Books, a division of HarperCollins Publishers, 10 East 53rd Street, New York, NY 10022.
www.harperteen.com

Library of Congress Cataloging-in-Publication Data
Davidson, Jenny.
Invisible things / Jenny Davidson. — 1st ed.
p. cm.
Sequel to: The explosionist.
Summary: In an alternate 1930s Europe, sixteen-year-old Sophie and Mikael, now more than a friend, investigate her parents' death, setting off a chain of events that unravels everything she thought she knew about her family, and involving them in international intrigue and the development of the atomic bomb.
ISBN 978-0-06-123978-6
[1. Family—Fiction. 2. Orphans—Fiction. 3. Scientists—Fiction. 4. Atomic bomb—Fiction. 5. Bohr, Niels, 1885–1962—Fiction. 6. Nobel, Alfred Bernhard, 1833–1896—Fiction.] I. Title.
PZ7.D28314Inv 2010 2010007032
[Fic]—dc22 CIP
AC

Typography by Andrea Vandergrift
10 11 12 13 14 CG/RRDB 10 9 8 7 6 5 4 3 2 1
❖
First Edition

In loving memory of Helen Hill,
and for Becky and Francis Pop

Prelude

7 October 1938

The Mansion of Honor

København, Denmark

Dusk came early at this time of year in Denmark. Together with the unseasonably heavy snow, the half darkness largely concealed the figure of a man balanced on the narrow ledge outside the grand windows of the conservatory at the Mansion of Honor, built by the owners of the Carlsberg Brewery as a home for Denmark's most distinguished citizen, the world-renowned physicist Niels Bohr.

Through the panes of glass, the man could see the hundreds of guests gathered to celebrate Bohr's birthday. He waited until the physicist himself had come into view, holding up a champagne flute for the birthday toasts. Then the man reached behind him, his glove brushing along the equipment tucked into his belt—grappling hooks, climbing rope, an electric torch—until it reached the sleek matte black rocket launcher.

Pressing the device up against the window, the man primed it and pulled the trigger.

Even as screams could be heard from party guests scrambling to get away from the device that now lay hissing in the middle of the conservatory, a cloud of gas beginning to fill the room and obscure its occupants, the man outside was letting himself down from the ledge, coiling up his rope, and making his swift way out through the grounds.

A black saloon with dark-tinted windows waited for him at the other side of the wall surrounding the estate. By the time the security officers had found the man's footprints and begun to follow his tracks, the car was long since off and away.

Part 1

August–October 1938

The Institute for Theoretical Physics

København, Denmark

20 August 1938

Dear Sophie:

Miss Henchman only would say that your great-aunt had sent you abroad, but there was an awful lot of rot talked before school finished about your having eloped with Mr. Petersen! I told the others it couldn't be so, but I still don't see why you left before sitting your exams—I am sure you would have done better than any of us. It is spiffy to be done with school forever—I have been assigned to a unit and will begin basic training at the end of the month. I should love to get a letter from you, Sophie—you might write to me in care of my parents, and they will forward it to my regiment. My father is certain that Scotland will go to war with Europe within the next few months, so there is a good chance I will see action before the winter. I take it that this is the best address for me to write you—but why on earth are you living at an Institute for Theoretical Physics? You always were a dark horse—I hope you are very well and that you will spare a thought now and again for

your loving friend,
Nan

Sophie was lying on her stomach on the bed in her own little room under the eaves, a bedroom with slanted walls and a small window overlooking the trees in the park behind the institute. As she read through Nan's letter for the third time, she blushed again at the bit about Mr. Petersen—she had once believed herself to be in love with the chemistry teacher, it was true, until the notion was dispelled by the revelation of her feelings for his younger brother, Mikael. Mikael had helped her escape from Scotland and the real danger that she would vanish into the labyrinth of an infernal training scheme instituted by Sophie's very own great-aunt and designed to brainwash young women, eroding their personalities and subtracting all freedom of will so as to subordinate them to the needs and desires of the country's most powerful men.

Mikael's mother, Fru Petersen, had worked for many years as housekeeper and general assistant to the institute's director, Niels Bohr; she managed purchasing and bookkeeping, ordered and cataloged books for the library, and made arrangements for visitors, including obtaining accommodations in nearby pensions or boardinghouses for anyone who could not be squeezed into the available space at the institute on Blegdamsvej. The Petersen family had long dwelled in one of four flats on the top floor of the institute, which had recently become Sophie's home also, at least for now, but the influx of scientists seeking refuge from the new European racial laws had placed an increasing strain on the institute's capacity to house them.

Nan's father was far from alone in his belief that war was imminent. After England had fallen to the European Federation during the Great War of the 1910s, the states of the New Hanseatic League (with Scotland, Denmark, and Estonia leading the way) had reached a precarious settlement with Europe, a settlement that had lasted decades, but the European Federation's dictatorial way of behaving within its borders and its territorial aggressiveness outside of them threatened to bring that peace to an end at any moment.

Sophie felt her own personal displacement more sharply than anything she read in the newspapers. The pale sandstone walls and clean lines of Niels Bohr's institute reminded her painfully of Edinburgh, and in general København struck her as uncannily familiar, though there were small particles of difference between the two cities that made one feel as though one had walked into a fairy-tale alternate universe: the red-tiled roofs, the abundance of bicycles in the streets, the ubiquity of cheese (creamy and crumbly, blue-veined, delicious) at breakfast.

None of this, though, was the sort of thing she could write in a letter to Nan, who was perhaps the least fanciful person Sophie had ever met in her life.

Just then she heard Mikael calling her name from below.

"Sophie! Come quickly; I need your help!"

Outside in the shrubbery, she found Mikael kneeling and trying to coax a small tabby cat from the undergrowth. He filled her in quickly on their task—half a dozen experimental subjects had escaped from the Hungarian chemist Georg de Hevesy's latest basement adventure in radioisotope research, a rogue macaw (survivor of a previous round of experimentation) having methodically unlatched the clasps on their cages. The cats had gone out through the window into the park that covered the whole tract of land behind the institute, and it was Mikael and Sophie's job to help round them up again.

Sophie crouched down and held out her hand to the small tabby, rubbing her forefingers against her thumb and making a sort of chirping noise.

The cat stared at her from deep in the undergrowth.

Meanwhile Mikael tiptoed in a wide circle around to the back of the bush. As he crept up on the creature, the cat pricked up its ears. A moment later, it had shot out of the brush, a striped blur in the far right of Sophie's field of vision.

Mikael swore. He had two brown canvas sacks tucked under his belt and held a third one open in his hands, which he let drop as Sophie joined him.

"It's hopeless," he said, wiping his brow with his sleeve.

"Let's try again over by the back wall of the park," Sophie suggested.

They tramped along the path toward the pond, stopping to splash their faces at the fountain along the way. This time they had better cat-catching luck. A small gray-and-white cat froze as Sophie approached, and Mikael had whisked it into the sack before the cat knew what was what.

The squirming and squalling of the now-animate bag sent Sophie into guilty fits of laughter. They called for Hevesy's assistant, Miss Levi, and left the sack lying in a spot of shade, then set off to stalk their next target. But as they approached the large black cat sunning himself on the top of the wall, Sophie put out a hand to hold Mikael back.

"It's Trismegistus, can't you see?" she whispered.

The red leather collar clearly identified the cat as Sophie and Mikael's former traveling companion. Mikael always just called the cat Blackie, but though Sophie found the name engraved on the collar's silver plate pretentious, she had a superstitious preference for using his proper name.

"Trismegistus!" she called.

The cat ignored her and simply went on grooming himself in the sun. The imposing creature's tenure as the favored intimate of a spiritualist medium—the woman whose murder earlier that summer in Edinburgh had indirectly led to Sophie's coming to live with Mikael and his mother in København—had given him a supreme degree of self-possession beyond even the usual lot of cats. He spent roughly half of his time indoors, often curled up in a compact mound at the foot of Sophie's bed, but he enjoyed preying on the population of small mammals and birds in the tame wilderness of the park.

Miss Levi had arrived by now and transferred the wriggling sack of cat into a wheelbarrow that already held several others.

"Will one of you come and help me inside?" she asked.

Mikael asserted the superiority of his own cat-catching prowess, so Sophie, after warning him that he would regret any attempt to exert it on Trismegistus, followed Miss Levi through the grounds to the back of the institute and right up to the service entrance.

The scientist unfastened the padlock on the door set horizontally into the ground, and together she and Sophie gently rolled the barrow down the ramp and up to the array of empty cages in the basement laboratory.

It was a tricky business to get each cat out of its sack and secured in a cage without injury to human or animal, but they managed it with only a few minor scratches.

"What should we do with them now?" Sophie asked.

She rather wished the escaped cats could have stayed escaped, but there was nothing to be gained by refusing to help round them up: some days earlier, they had been injected with a radioactive isotope of phosphorus whose uptake into the skeleton could be measured with great precision, revealing how bone was formed and all sorts of other metabolic secrets. Sophie and Mikael both helped out regularly in the basement laboratory, and Sophie knew the cats' doom was already sealed. When the time came, the animals would be euthanized and samples of their bone and tissue burned or dissolved in acid so that the precipitated phosphate could be weighed and tested for radioactivity, using a "clicker" or counter that had been modified from the ones the telephone company used to track how many calls were made on a given line.

"Now we must test them," Miss Levi answered, "to see which ones are ours."

"Can't you tell just by looking at them?" said Sophie.

"Oh, no," Miss Levi said. "I can make a good guess, certainly, but since it's a matter of life or death for these poor little fellows, I had rather be certain."

"What will we do with the ones who weren't in the experiment?" Sophie asked, feeling slightly sick to her stomach.

"We'll release them back into the park," said Miss Levi—she had told Sophie to call her Hilde, and she wasn't at all old, but Sophie felt more comfortable with "Miss Levi"—"but not until we've made a very thorough attempt to retrieve all six of the ones that escaped. There's no point chasing after the same cats all over again!"

It was certainly a two-person job to work out which cats were radioactive. Sophie put on a pair of heavy gardening gloves and held down an animal while Miss Levi briskly pinched each cat's jaw with one hand and swabbed its mouth for saliva with the other. The wipe test was then passed under the clicker, which went alarmingly active in several cases, including the little gray-and-white cat, which Sophie had hoped might be spared.

They had determined that two of the five captured cats belonged to the original group when Hevesy himself entered the room. He had a charming long face like a dyspeptic turtle, with a slender build and a patina of formality to his manners that made Sophie suspect him of being privately quite sarcastic. As always, he was dressed in an elegant fashion that went against the otherwise casual sartorial culture of the institute, but his brow was dotted anomalously with sweat. He held a bloodstained white silk handkerchief to his left hand, and his clothes bore the marks of the hunt.

Miss Levi clucked over him as she examined the deep slash on the mound of his thumb.

"I take it you couldn't keep hold of the animal?" she asked.

"I got him, all right," said Hevesy. "I left the bag outside because the creature was writhing about too powerfully for me to keep hold of it. I deposited the sack in one of the garden rubbish bins and came to you, Miss Levi, for assistance."

"I'll go out and get it, Miss Levi," Sophie volunteered. The feeling of moral queasiness based on complicity with scientific cat killing had given way, over the course of Hevesy's utterances, to a more specific and acute sense of dismay. She left by the garden entrance and half ran, with the slight limp that was the only physical legacy of the injury she had sustained in the long-ago factory explosion that had killed both her parents, to the garden refuse bins.

One bin was rocking about on its base, an anguished and barely muffled yowl emanating from the container. Sophie removed the lid and grasped the neck of the sack with both hands. It was like trying to hold on to a portion of volcanic magma the size of a plum pudding. Clutching the sack, she felt something punch her quite painfully round about the kidney.

Once she had passed the malevolent bundle over to Miss Levi, the laboratory assistant barely had time to loosen the neck of the sack, pop it through the cage's opening, and slam the door shut before the cat shot out like a rocket and slammed into the wire wall at the back of the cage.

"It's Trismegistus!" Sophie cried, her pangs of guilt intensified by the black cat's sheer physical fury. If he could have stabbed Sophie with a knife, she thought, he would have!

"It's *what?*" Hevesy asked, the smooth surface of his politeness slightly dented by the cat's awful yowling.

"It's the cat that came with me from Scotland. Look, he's got a red collar; none of yours had a collar—oh, please, let him out at once!"

A cursory visual examination confirmed the truth of Sophie's words.

"Still," Miss Levi said sensibly, "it will be more prudent to keep him here for now and let him back out only once we have found the others. . . ."

The cat was howling so loudly by this time that the other animals in the room had become agitated.

"Oh, please don't say that!" Sophie said. "Really, we must let him go—look how he's upsetting the others!"

This had to be conceded. Even the macaw was fluttering off his perch and screaming, and the cats were making an extraordinary amount of noise.

"I am not so sure," said Miss Levi, giving the cat a wary look, "that it will be quite *safe* for us to release him inside. Sophie, what do you think?"

The cat seemed also to turn his gaze now in Sophie's direction, and the thought came very strongly into her mind that he would prefer to be released outdoors, but not at the cost of significant further delay. The cage had two handles, and she hoisted it up in both hands and hurried over and up the stairs out into the garden.

Despite her haste and the enveloping sensation of panic, Sophie placed the cage carefully on the grass and knelt down in front of it.

"Oh, I do hope you will forgive me," she said, though she felt very silly even as she uttered the words. "I'm terribly sorry you had to go through all this!"

Once the door was open, though, the cat stalked out with a dignity quite at odds with his earlier cannonball-like activity. He slowly picked up speed, first to a brisk trot and then to a low sprint that took him into the invisibility-granting world of the park's dense undergrowth.

After supper with Mikael and Fru Petersen, Sophie had a quick bath to wash away the grime of cat chasing. Dressed in her pajamas, she joined Mikael in the small sitting room. It was still light outside, but the evening had become quite cool. Summer was over.

Fru Petersen brought them each a mug of cocoa and waved away Mikael's invitation to sit down.

"I am going to bed," she said firmly. "I am not fifteen years old; I prefer to go to bed at a reasonable hour, even if it *is* Saturday tomorrow. . . ."

Once she had left them, silence fell over the room. Sophie and Mikael sat across from each other on the two upholstered chairs. It seemed to Sophie that they hewed to an unspoken agreement at home that even the slightest physical contact was forbidden, though outside Mikael had more than once taken Sophie's hand and held it gently in his own for a few moments as they walked along together.

Sophie considered this almost heart-stoppingly bold. What if someone saw them? Would Mikael really not mind people thinking Sophie was his—what was the right word?—sweetheart, and he Sophie's beau?

Her thoughts roamed to the laboratory downstairs.

"Did you ever think it might be wrong," she asked Mikael, "to keep animals in cages and do things to them that would be considered unacceptable if they weren't directed toward scientific ends?"

"It's crossed my mind," Mikael admitted. He slurped the last dregs of his cocoa—how had he finished his so much more quickly than Sophie?—and set the mug down on the end table. "We eat animals, too, though, don't we? And wear leather shoes and jackets and belts? Experiments like those ones they're doing in the basement are almost the only way to come to grips with even the most elementary aspects of physiology, in humans as well as animals—it's not possible, after all, to experiment on people!"

"No, of course not," Sophie said, "and I know that Professor Hevesy is engaged in truly important research; only I hope that his next experiment does not require him to kill so many dear little cats!"

As if his appearance had been scripted, the black cat materialized in the doorway, wedging the door a little wider open and weaving his way around the edge of the room toward Sophie. He rubbed his muzzle along the hand she offered him, then sprang up onto the arm of the chair and settled down in the pose preferred by the Egyptian sphinxes.

"He is amazingly intelligent, isn't he?" Sophie said, giving the cat a series of strong, firm strokes over his brow ridges and ears, a form of patting that made the cat purr like a dynamo.

"Hevesy?"

"No!"

"Oh, you're talking about Blackie. . . ."

Sophie gave Mikael a reproachful look, and he started to laugh.

"I suppose you wish I'd call him Trismegistus! But it's a ridiculous name for a cat, Sophie; it makes the wretched beast sound like the prop of some charlatan of an occult practitioner. Just because he once belonged to a spiritualist medium doesn't mean he's not a perfectly ordinary, common-or-garden-variety black cat! Bet you he prefers to be called Blackie—look! Here, Blackie, do you want the last bit of cocoa?"

He picked up the mug and held it about a foot from the ground, tipping it forward in the cat's direction and jiggling it to slosh the scant remaining liquid around at the bottom. The cat remained impervious to the cocoa's charms, perhaps because of the affront to his dignity, but more likely because Fru Petersen had already given him herring for supper; Sophie could still slightly smell the residue on his face and whiskers, though he was an irreproachably clean cat who groomed himself at every opportunity and sported an exceptionally thick and glossy coat.

"I agree it's a bit silly," Sophie said regretfully, "but really I think he must be called Trismegistus. It suits him, in a slightly sinister way. Perhaps he wouldn't object to being called Tris for short. What do you think, Tris?"

When she reached under his chin and began rubbing along the bottom of his jaw, his purring swelled to such a degree that Mikael could hear it all the way on the other side of the room.

"Tris it is, then," he said, with a sigh of resignation so dramatic that Sophie couldn't help but laugh.

In the absence of anything better to do—his mother would be very annoyed if she saw the mess!—Mikael was plucking the white blossoms off a flowering branch that Fru Petersen had arranged in a sleek white modern vase. The petals mounted in a heap, Mikael registering what he had been doing only when every twig had been stripped bare of blossom; he looked surprised, then picked up the pile of petals in both hands and heaved himself out of his chair to cast them in Sophie's direction.

The petals descended over Sophie and the cat like snow.

With the last petals still fluttering to the ground, Mikael's mother leaned her head around the door.

"Still up?" she said. "You two had a long day—I'd say it's bedtime around now. What a mess you've made!"

Sophie cleaned her teeth in the bathroom. Mikael had taken to leaving his toothbrush and the little tin of cleaning powder by the kitchen sink and brushing his teeth there to avoid either enduring or instigating a bathroom wait; Sophie would have been glad to let him go first in the bathroom, but Mikael's notion of the obligations of the guest-host relationship entwined the pair of them in a merciless web of mutual courtesies.

She left her door open a crack, and a few minutes after she had turned out the bedside light, Trismegistus padded into the room and jumped up onto the bed with the funny little revving-up noise that Sophie found so endearing.

She turned onto her side, and the cat tucked himself into the space between her arms and stomach like a hot, fat, furry sausage. The cat's companionship was one of Sophie's greatest consolations in her new Danish life. It wasn't a bad life, on its own terms, but it had made all of the futures her past self had spent so much time pondering go quite blank.

All she seemed able to do now was wait. When would the dynamiteur Alfred Nobel send word that he was ready to see Sophie? Just before she'd left Scotland, she'd spoken to Nobel on the telephone, and he had promised all sorts of revelations about Sophie's long-dead parents, but she had never expected such a long time to pass before his next communication. When Nobel did finally reach out to her, would the message be brought by her old chemistry teacher, Mikael's older brother, Arne?

Would Mikael—but Sophie could hardly stand to think about it, the idea so thoroughly and confusingly excited and shamed her—ever want to kiss her?

Just then the cat reached out his left paw and laid it on Sophie's forearm, kneading her flesh for a moment and giving her a short, sharp dig with his claws.

"Stop that!" Sophie said, outraged and rolling away from him.

No sooner had she turned her back than the cat raised himself up and picked his way around the blanketed outline of her body to set himself back down along Sophie's front.

"I do not see why you have to lie on my front side," she said with fond exasperation, but the cat only purred and settled himself closer by.

For Saturday-morning breakfast, Mikael's mother always made them crepes filled with apricot jam and sprinkled with powdered sugar, which seemed almost criminally delicious for a meal that in Sophie's Scottish life had usually been more penitential than mouthwatering—oh, but she must stop making these comparisons! Even when the advantage fell to København, as often seemed the case, there was something reproach-worthy about looking constantly backward. It was better not to let the words *In Scotland* . . . or *At home* . . . ever cross her lips; it was the lesson of Orpheus and Eurydice, or of Lot's wife looking back and being turned into a pillar of salt.

After helping with the washing-up (and *goodness*, it was nice having hot running water and electric wiring—but there she went with another "In Edinburgh"!), Sophie spent an hour on her history essay. Mikael went to the boys' school where Niels Bohr had sent his sons, but Sophie had been enrolled as a pupil at a very good English-language coeducational school founded and directed by Bohr's aunt Hanna Adler. Sophie liked the Fællesskole quite a bit. It was a progressive school, which seemed mostly to mean that children so inclined were allowed to behave very badly, but that lessons were considerably more interesting than at an ordinary school. All but the most daunting teachers were called by their first names, a custom Sophie judged strange but pleasant: the verdict she had reached on almost every aspect of her new life.

At the other side of the dining table, Mikael was covering sheets of paper with intricate penciled calculations, and the example of his easy concentration helped Sophie become fully absorbed in her own essay, which was on the relationship between aboveboard diplomacy and secret operations like espionage or even assassination.

In a way it was like animal vivisection or scientific experimentation. Sophie would much prefer not to euthanize and dissect an animal with her own two hands. Just so might she recoil at the notion of ordering an assassination, let alone assassinating someone herself. But there was a kind of hypocrisy, wasn't there, in congratulating oneself on not having to descend to such things while simultaneously benefiting from living in a world where espionage and even assassination might be the only way for one's country to maintain its independence?

She finished a paragraph and started doodling in the margin of the page. Drawing a blank as to what to say next, she decided to consult the encyclopedia, whose gilded black-and-red volumes took up almost a whole shelf in the library downstairs. On a weekday, a noisy game of Ping-Pong might have been under way at the table by the library windows, which were always kept open to clear the haze of tobacco smoke that otherwise hung in the air; the cold air had led someone to put a joke sign above the door (but it would make more sense when winter came!) saying NORDPOL, with *North Pole* written underneath for English speakers, and one of the eccentric Russian George Gamow's trademark drawings of Bohr as Mickey Mouse. Bohr/Mickey was dressed up as Father Christmas and brandished a Ping-Pong racquet at his team of reindeer; it was one of the great mysteries of life how the crude inked figure could so clearly represent all three things at once—Bohr, Mickey, Father Christmas.

Today being Saturday, the library was empty. Leafing her way through to *Intelligence Services,* Sophie got distracted by *Ichneumon, Ichthyology,* and *Iodine,* and she was immersed in *Ice (glacial)* when someone tapped her on the shoulder.

It was Niels Bohr himself. After checking that Sophie did not mind the interruption, he pulled up a chair, tipped back in it, and rested his feet on the table in front of them.

Bohr was kind to everybody, in his own absentminded

fashion, but the great surprise of Sophie's first days in København a month earlier had come when Mikael's mother informed her that Bohr wished to see Sophie in his office.

Sophie had flinched—it sounded distinctly disciplinary!—whereupon Fru Petersen twisted her mouth in a comical fashion and said, "The only person who is not periodically summoned to the great man's office is the janitor, and that is because Bohr knows the fellow will only importune him for more funds if they meet face-to-face!"

"What does Professor Bohr want to talk to me about?" Sophie asked, but Fru Petersen couldn't give her an answer.

So Sophie had duly appeared in the outer sanctuary, the secretary asking her to sit quietly until Bohr was ready to see her. Her heart had been in her mouth as she waited, and she felt almost breathless with nerves. Would he cross-examine her about her visa status, or, worse, about her fairly sketchy knowledge of nuclear physics?

But when she was finally ushered into Bohr's office, Sophie had seen not an ogre but a kind-faced man whose boyish manner belied the fact of his being in late middle age. The first thing he did was jump out of his seat and rush over to Sophie and clasp her hands in his own, leaning over to look closely into her face.

"A definite resemblance," he muttered. "It would be an exaggeration to say I'd have known you anywhere—it is difficult to pick out a likeness in the face of a complete stranger on the street—but I see quite a strong look of your father. . . ."

Seeing the puzzled expression on Sophie's face, he led her to a phalanx of framed photographs on the wall beside the window. There was a row of almost indistinguishable group portraits of the institute's staff—the earliest ones had only twelve or fourteen people in them, while the more recent ones were populated by several dozen figures—and there in the back right-hand corner of the group photograph for the year 1917 was Sophie's very own father, who had died (so had her mother) when she was too young to remember him.

"Alan came to the institute as a postdoctoral fellow in 1912," Bohr had told Sophie. Then he put his finger to the smudge of a half-visible face of a young woman standing at the other edge of the group. She had turned away, as if responding to a comment from someone outside the frame of the picture, and there was something elusive—almost ghostly—about her equivocal presence. "Your mother had already been working here for a year when he came, but it took him many months to persuade her to let him take her out for coffee and cake!"

Sophie had been struck almost dumb with surprise.

"My mother and father met *here?*" she had asked, after recovering her voice. "At the Institute for Theoretical Physics?"

"Did you not know?" Bohr had said in response, frowning a little and opening a drawer from which he extracted a tin of biscuits. Taking the lid off, he had offered it to Sophie, who chose a rectangular shortbread, and then he himself carefully picked out two chocolate-covered round ones dusted with coconut. He had gone on to tell Sophie the tale of Alan Hunter's courtship of a shy, charming fellow Scot called Rose Childs, a story hitherto entirely unknown to Sophie, before further endearing himself to her by offering her some fudge from the secret supply in his office cupboard. He had concluded by telling her that *Sophie* had been a favorite name of his ever since his time as a very junior research fellow in Manchester, when he had taught himself English by reading *David Copperfield* and looking up the words he didn't recognize. "Dickens's Sophie," he had added, "lived in Devonshire and was one of ten, as I am sure you know!"

Seeing Bohr again now in the library, the pages of her history essay slightly fluttering (she had pinned them down with a malachite paperweight) in the breeze from the windows, Sophie had to fight the urge to pepper him with more questions about her parents. But though she desperately wanted to learn everything she could, she did not want Bohr to think of Sophie as a person of exclusively genealogical interests. It was hard to shake the sense instilled by her stern guardian, Great-aunt Tabitha, an elderly lady of supreme rectitude who had seen fit to keep Sophie almost entirely in the dark about her antecedents, that questions about one's deceased parents represented idle curiosity of the most frivolous sort.

The encyclopedia volume still open before her, she asked Bohr the question that had been troubling her as she wrote her essay.

"Say that someone's leading a double life," she began, remembering not just Great-aunt Tabitha and her twin role as enlightener and secret keeper for the sinister organization called IRYLNS, but also Sophie's former history teacher, Miss Chatterjee, and Arne Petersen himself, and the ways their secrets deformed and distorted their other human relationships. When Mikael's older brother had posed as Sophie's chemistry teacher in Edinburgh, he had really been working as a secret agent for the reclusive dynamiteur Alfred Nobel. It had taken Sophie quite a long time to apprehend the extent of Arne's double-dealing, and to add insult to injury, after revealing to Sophie that Nobel had actually connived at a plan to bring Sophie to see him in his . . . Sophie mentally supplied the word *lair*, Arne had simply gone off without doing *anything* about making arrangements for a visit that Sophie perhaps dreaded and looked forward to in equal measure.

"Would you say that it is possible for each strand of that life to be full of integrity," she asked Bohr, "even if it is lived under conditions of concealment? Or does the ongoing deception tarnish the person's character regardless, even if each strand of the life seems respectable on its own?"

"Do I detect a question motivated by something other than abstract curiosity?" Bohr asked, his voice kind. He snapped the book shut and took his pipe from his breast pocket, then began the near-interminable process of fiddling that might or might not culminate half an hour later in its finally being lit. "Are you thinking of Arne Petersen?"

Sophie flushed and nodded.

"Do you think I'll hear from him soon about the visit to Mr. Nobel?" she asked Bohr, hating how pitiful she sounded but unable to stop the words from tumbling out of her mouth.

"I hope so," Bohr said apologetically, "but it is honestly impossible to say. You know that the institute gets a good deal of its funding from Nobel's various trusts and foundations; at times I will receive from the man as many as three or four telegrams in a single morning, whereas at other times months may pass without a hint of response even to my most pressing inquiries. It can be highly frustrating, but then that is the price we pay when we deal with these great men. . . ."

He did not seem to use the phrase ironically, and it caused Sophie to bristle slightly on Bohr's own behalf. Surely Bohr himself was by any rational standard of measurement as great a man as Alfred Nobel!

Just then Mikael peered around the door of the library.

"There you are, Sophie!" he called out. "Professor Bohr, I must claim Sophie for a bicycle ride. . . ."

"We just as well could ride later on, though, couldn't we?" Sophie said hopefully.

Mikael started laughing, and so did Bohr—alas, bicycle riding was one of the minor banes of Sophie's Danish existence, and it was well-known throughout the institute that Sophie would have been very glad had the bicycle never been invented.

As they clattered downstairs through the deserted building, Sophie had an appealing sense of the institute's being their own personal playground. The main building, in addition to the residential flats and guest rooms on the top floor, held laboratory and office space for about fifteen physicists. The ground floor had a big office and reception area for Bohr and his secretary, and an auditorium that could seat almost a hundred people. The basement, served by a goods elevator, housed a chemical laboratory and four big workrooms for experimental research. It was packed full of all sorts of things whose inner workings Sophie did not always fully understand but whose names rolled off the tongue in a most lovely way: a high-tension generator, a grating spectrograph, a precision lathe, drills and saws and sanders, and the delightfully named universal cutting machine. Of course, the universal cutting machine could not really cut *everything*; it was just a name, but Sophie liked the notion that it might be used to cut out a neat strip of sky or a perfect cube of water.

And in a detail like something out of a fairy tale, a seven-meter well had been dug deep below the floor of the basement, with a narrow staircase leading down into it. It had been built for the spectrograph, which had been floated at the bottom of the well in a container of oil meant to minimize vibrations from the trolley cars that ran along Blegdamsvej in front of the institute, but when the vibrations continued to affect the instrument, it had to be moved elsewhere. Now the underground cave was used to produce and store the radioactive isotopes for Hevesy's tracer experiments, the Hungarian scientist's slight resemblance to a turtle only compounding Sophie's sense of its being a magical grotto where frogs might turn into princes if the right person kissed them.

The bicycle shed stood on the east side of the building. By the time Sophie had knocked over several other machines and barked her shins painfully on the lawn mower, Mikael was already riding around outside in circles.

It was not so much that Sophie minded actually riding a bicycle. It was quite enjoyable, really, once one was rolling along, so long as one did not allow oneself to become flustered when a dog took chase or a small child rushed directly out into one's path. But bicycles themselves were so troublesome and awkward! One banged one's shins on them and knocked into things as one tried to wheel them out of congested areas, and it still seemed to Sophie impossible to imagine walking and wheeling the wretched contraption at anything like a normal pace.

Intent upon her dislike for two-wheeled transportation, Sophie remained almost oblivious to the route Mikael led them along, except to think that it was a pity the weather was fair and København so attractive, because it led to excessive numbers of people being out and about enjoying themselves and altogether neglecting the possibility that their obstruction of the path of a timid cyclist might pose some danger to themselves and others!

She was taken aback when she realized they had already reached the pier.

"It's not much of a ride," Mikael observed as they stretched their legs out in front of them on the sun-warmed dock and unpacked their lunch. This was the magnificent imperial bit of København, almost everything built on a monumental scale.

"It is a nice little bicycle; I will give you that much," Sophie said, feeling more charitable now that the first part of the ride was over. Mikael loved riding his bike, and had insisted that Sophie must have her own, persuading his mother to mention it to Great-aunt Tabitha, who had wired the money to purchase one just for Sophie, Mikael having rightly noted that there were few things so unhelpful to the timid cyclist as trying to ride a bicycle the wrong size, and that though the institute shed might be full of more or less functional hand-me-downs, they had all been ridden by much taller people than Sophie.

It was blue, Sophie's favorite color. Mikael had fixed a block to the left pedal to neutralize the leg-length discrepancy Sophie had retained from her childhood injury. Perhaps, in time—in a very *long* time—she might even learn to love the bicycle?

Mikael offered Sophie a sandwich, which she took and washed down with a swig of lemonade from the bottle. A number of other people were also enjoying proximity to the water, mostly families with children eating ice creams or couples holding hands. Sophie sneaked a glance at Mikael, but it did not really seem as though he was thinking about reaching out for her hand. Just in case, though, she wiped her right hand surreptitiously on her shorts to reduce stickiness.

Amidst the generally companionable scene, solitary walkers were relatively conspicuous, especially because they all seemed to be men in suits, several of them carrying briefcases or at least a rolled newspaper tucked beneath the elbow. Sophie was only idly watching, but she saw one man sit down at the end of a bench, at the other end of which an older gentleman was already sitting reading the paper. After a moment, the older man folded up his paper and left it beside him on the bench, then walked away in the direction of Christiansborg. The other man waited a few minutes, then stood up himself, plucking the paper from the seat without even looking at it, tucking it under his own arm, and walking away in the opposite direction from the first man.

Mikael had been following the direction of Sophie's gaze.

"Spies," he announced breezily, enjoying the effect the word had on Sophie.

"Spies?" she breathed. When espionage was the topic for a history essay, it might seem slightly dreary, but the idea of seeing a real actual spy was singularly romantic. "How do you know?"

"Well, obviously the second man was there to pick up some sort of document from the first," Mikael said. "That's how they teach them to do it at spy school! It's called a drop, and the newspaper exchange is one of the most basic ways of handing something over. Not that there's anything wrong with keeping it simple. . . ."

"But if it's really secret," Sophie said, "why do they do it in broad daylight and in such a public place?"

"I suppose the rationale is that some things are best hidden in plain sight," said Mikael. "It's impossible to keep secrets in a city this size anyway. Nobody's supposed to know who the spies are, but really it's incredibly obvious: they're all either attached to a legation, with some nominal cover-up title like *cultural attaché*, or else they pretend to be correspondents for Reuters or one of the other wire services. They spend most of their time going to parties at the other consulates, and it's all fairly civilized, although I suppose that will change if the Hanseatic states really go to war with Europe."

"Is war quite inevitable, do you think?" Sophie asked.

"If I were judging based on what I read in the newspapers and hear on the radio, no," Mikael said, "but Professor Bohr seems to think it's almost certain, and he knows all sorts of things we don't. Scandinavia's been simply crawling with European agents for the last few years; that's nothing new—just yesterday Bohr got a postcard from our old lodger Ludwig Wittgenstein. You know, Sophie, he's the fellow who built that tiny working model of a sewing machine out of matchsticks, the one that's on the dresser in your room. Wittgenstein said that a German woman spy had been spotted near his retreat in the remote northern bit of Norway, and what gave her away was the fact that she was wearing trousers, though I don't really see how that follows—surely a woman who was not a spy might wear trousers also? When he lived here, Wittgenstein was often ranting about his dislike for women in trousers, so perhaps it is a biased account! But these days it seems as though Denmark's become a sort of espionage hub for the whole world, with all of the English and French and German and Russian agents hanging around here till the show gets going."

Sophie's eye wandered a little farther down the pier. Her gaze snagged on the figure of a man sitting on a bench on the far side of the next ice-cream kiosk. He was eating an apple and reading a magazine.

"Mikael?" she asked, feeling slightly breathless.

"What?"

"It might be that I am just shortsighted—but doesn't that fellow look awfully like your brother?"

"Oh, but it couldn't be; Arne isn't anywhere near here—Arne!"

Mikael took off running toward the man eating the apple, leaving Sophie stuck with not just one but *both* bicycles, wretched encumbrances that they were! She had to wait, fuming, for Mikael to reach his brother and pull him to his feet and give him a highly continental kiss on both cheeks; Sophie slightly squirmed at the knowledge of having imbibed one of her great-aunt's prejudices against the customs of what Great-aunt Tabitha always referred to as *foreigners*.

Soon they were headed back in Sophie's direction.

"But why didn't you say you were coming?" she cried out

once she and Arne had exchanged greetings.

"I wasn't sure I'd be able to get away until quite late last night," Arne said. "I took the train and the ferry and then another train—got in first thing this morning, and had to see a man about a dog before I could look you up."

He spoke with a certain evasive jauntiness that irritated Sophie. Clearly Mikael felt much the same way, for he wrinkled his nose at his brother and said, "Well, aren't *you* full of yourself these days! Coming back to the institute?"

Arne agreed that yes, he did mean to spend the night at home. He had no luggage to speak of, only a small khaki-colored rucksack, and after some experimentation, the two brothers found a way to fit themselves both on the bicycle, with Mikael pedaling and Arne crouched on the rack behind him.

Back at the institute, Mikael and Sophie left their bicycles in the shed (Sophie gave hers a guilty farewell pat on the seat, an apology for insufficient fondness—all she could think about was whether Arne had brought any message for her from Alfred Nobel!) and climbed the stairs with Arne in front of them.

On their way down the hall to the flat, they heard voices coming from the lunchroom under the eaves. Mikael and Sophie both sped up—it had been firmly impressed upon Sophie from childhood not to intrude where business was being conducted—but Arne put up his hand to stop them, then pushed the door farther open and beckoned to them to follow.

The lunchroom was one of Sophie's favorite rooms at the institute. It had been a surprise, on first arriving here, to find that there was no cafeteria; Sophie had imagined that the institute, like a school or hospital, would have a dreary refectory with a line of ladies slopping awful hot food onto trays. But Denmark was a nation of boxed lunches. Almost everyone who worked at the institute brought a packed lunch from home or lodgings, supplemented in the lunchroom by hot coffee and a generous supply of bread and cheese and apples. One of the English refugees even kept a tin well stocked with biscuits, though crunching into a custard cream or a shortbread filled Sophie with such sharp nostalgia that she would almost rather forgo the treat.

As it was Saturday, there wasn't any bread and cheese laid out, but a fresh pot of coffee had just been brewed, and Bohr was pouring it into sturdy china cups for his two companions, Lise Meitner and Otto Robert Frisch.

"Hello, Arne," Frisch said cheerfully. "Haven't seen you for a while; are you here for the weekend?"

Though Arne gave his assent, Bohr hardly seemed to notice anyone had come into the room.

"What if the repulsive force of the high surface charge

of the uranium nucleus turns out to cancel the attractive force of the surface tension?" he was saying. "There would be vibrations; instability would ensue!"

Quite a bit of coffee went into the saucers as he gesticulated, and Frisch kindly took the jug from Bohr's hands to finish pouring. In the meantime, Bohr transferred three or four heaping spoonfuls of sugar into his own cup and absently plucked a chocolate biscuit from the open tin, breaking it into pieces and consuming it in bits as he continued to talk.

One of the things that most amazed Sophie about the institute was the unending stream of conversation, conversation exceptional in its quality as well as its quantity. Bohr seemed to think best in the company of others, a mode of operating that Sophie found intriguing but strange, and he conducted himself during these endless conversations with an utter lack of reserve. The scientists Sophie remembered from her great-aunt's Edinburgh coffee evenings had often been tight-lipped to the point of paranoia, perhaps due to the Scottish preference for the laconic over the lavishly verbal, but talk here was a matter of almost divine candor and openness.

"Assuming the nucleus splits into two parts," Lise Meitner said in response to Bohr's observation, "the split-up would be accompanied by a transformation of rest mass into kinetic energy on the order of two hundred million electron volts."

Professor Meitner was rather Sophie's hero. They had

scarcely exchanged a dozen words, though the professor always gave Sophie a shy smile in the corridor, but the fact of a woman being among this august company as a full and equal colleague made Sophie's heart thrill with the spirit of emulation. Hilde Levi, whom Sophie also looked up to but who was junior enough not to produce quite the same effect of overwhelming awe, had told Sophie an amazing story about the working conditions Lise Meitner had experienced in Berlin before the new racial laws—implemented first in Germany, but now being leveled throughout France, Spain, and most of southern Europe also—made it impossible for her to keep her university appointment. The Chemical Institute had been off-limits to women, and Lise Meitner was only grudgingly allowed to use a basement carpenter's room that had a separate entrance to the street. She couldn't go upstairs to the institute, not even to her collaborator's laboratory, and when she needed to use the toilet, she had to walk to a café nearby. She was paid no salary for the work she did there, and lived only by eking out an allowance from her parents in a small furnished room in an unattractive neighborhood at the end of a tram line. The work she had done under these conditions, however, had earned her a Nobel Prize.

"Shouldn't we go?" Sophie whispered to Mikael.

He shrugged.

"Arne seems interested," he said to her under his breath,

"and I would bet that Professor Bohr hasn't even noticed we're here!"

"Lise Meitner is correct," said Frisch in response to the female scientist's observation about the transformation of mass into energy. He was Meitner's nephew, but perhaps to avoid the appearance of family bias always scrupulously referred to her by her full name. "We intend to observe the ionization pulses from the fragments of the . . . oh, what's a better word for it? We can't keep using this term *split-up*; it's too slangy."

"There is a closely analogous process in biology," Bohr interjected. "You English speakers"—cocking his head at Sophie and Mikael; so he did know that they were there!—"what would you call the process by which bacteria divide in two?"

"Do you mean fission?" Sophie asked uncertainly. English was the lingua franca of the institute, with bits of Danish and French and German mixed in, with the result that as a native English speaker one never quite knew whether one were stating something too obvious to be worth mentioning or so obscure as to defy comprehension.

"*Nuclear fission,* that will be an extremely suitable name," said Lise Meitner, making a note in her diary and giving Sophie an approving nod.

Bohr seemed hardly to have been paying attention. He

had eaten half a dozen chocolate biscuits—he had an insatiable appetite for sweets, especially chocolate. Now he bounded up out of his seat, taking his tobacco pouch out of his pocket and beginning to fiddle with his pipe.

"If we record the size of the pulse with enough accuracy," Lise Meitner added, "we will certainly be able to determine the energy groups and the mode of division."

Bohr stopped in his tracks. The lit match went out.

"Oh, what idiots we have all been!" he cried out. "But this is wonderful; this is just as it must be! You and Otto must write a paper—you will send it to *Nature*; I will read it for you first. . . ."

Nature was still perhaps the premier scientific journal of the entire world, though its editors had been forced to move their office from London to the Channel Islands in the 1910s, their evacuation only just preceding Europe's successful invasion of England. It was certainly Sophie's favorite out of all the journals readily accessible in the library downstairs—it did not have the more recondite charms of *Chemical News* or the *Annals of Physical Chemistry*, but on the other hand one could actually understand most of the articles.

Meanwhile the aunt and nephew were exchanging looks of amusement. Often time lagged between Bohr's hearing something and his really and truly understanding it, so that if one did not know better, one might have taken him almost for an idiot.

As the conversation veered off into the logistics of who would write what when, its appeal for Arne seemed to weaken; he motioned to Sophie and Mikael, and they traipsed after him down the hall to the family flat, where Fru Petersen first smacked Arne with the wooden spoon she was holding and berated him for not saying that he was coming, then enfolded him in her arms.

"Tonight we will have a feast," Mikael happily predicted to Sophie. They had been sent off to the shops with a long list of provisions, including large quantities of butter and almonds and confectioner's sugar, promising items from a cake-related standpoint.

It was curious. Fru Petersen was almost alone among grown-ups of Sophie's acquaintance in disapproving of Nobel and what he stood for. She was not opposed to the manufacture of weapons as such, but the name of Alfred Nobel had come to be associated (it was highly ironic!) not just with a paradoxical pacifism but with a radical antiwar cartel that did not draw the line even at the assassination of a minister of state if that person seemed to stand in the way of peace. Sophie had given up trying to understand the logic of pacifism's being yoked to a violent political ideology, but she was very glad that Fru Petersen had reconsidered her hard-line position on the morality of being in touch with a son who worked for the Nobel Consortium.

Supper was pleasant enough but rather tense. Sophie found it mildly salutary to have her own perhaps overly rose-colored views of family life washed into a more plausibly grimy hue by the palette of interactions at the Petersen dining table. After the meal, which had left everyone feeling rather too full and suffering from the closeness of the air under the eaves, Mikael sat straight up in his chair.

"I know what we should do!" he said. "Mother, you know we haven't been to swim in Sortedamsø at all this summer—you wouldn't mind if we slipped over there for a quick dip, would you?"

"You're not meant to swim there outside of the summer months, and we're well into September," Fru Petersen said, though Sophie could tell she wasn't wholeheartedly against the idea.

"Oh, do let's, though!" Mikael said. "It may well be the last night that's warm enough—the weather's sure to turn any day now."

"Sophie, are you a fairly strong swimmer?" Fru Petersen asked. "You mustn't go if you don't think you'll be safe."

"Strong enough, I think," said Sophie, who counted swimming as one of her few genuine enthusiasms on the athletic side of things. She had learned to swim in the heated saltwater lido on the cliffs at North Berwick, and had never been daunted by the chilly air and relatively cool waters of Scotland's eastern coast. She was more enthusiastic than skillful or speedy, but she could swim a strong and steady crawl, the Australian stroke whose introduction into the northern hemisphere by the glamorous Annette Kellerman had led to the industrialist Henry Ford's seeing Kellerman swim in a display tank in Detroit (Sophie had watched a very good film about this once) and falling in love with her and courting her by designing an amphibious vehicle in which they departed from their wedding reception on the island of Alcatraz, with the vehicle itself later reaching its apotheosis as the mass-produced sea-to-land tank/boat hybrid that would play the decisive role in the Californian war against Mexico.

Wearing their bathing costumes under their clothes, they walked over to the canal. A surprising number of other pedestrians were out and about in the streets, taking advantage of the last of the warm weather.

A footpath ran the whole length of the three kilometers of the canal known as Sortedamsø, and several bridges crossed it at various points, but even at its narrowest, it was still at least a hundred and fifty meters across, and for the most part closer to two hundred.

Mikael and his brother stripped down to their trunks. Sophie turned away from them, pulled her dress over her head, and folded it neatly beside her leather sandals. She slipped into the water without looking in the direction of the others, hoping that they, too, had done her the courtesy of turning their eyes away.

She yelped a little at the feeling of the cold water on her skin, but really it was lovely. She windmilled to warm up her arms and legs, then rolled over onto her back and lay there floating and looking up at the starry skies above.

Arne struck out almost immediately in the lengthwise direction of the canal, but Mikael and Sophie, in unspoken agreement, set out together at a more moderate pace across its width. They rested at the other side and caught their breath for a minute before swimming back over to where they had gotten in.

Mikael's brother was long gone by now. They could not even hear the quiet *splish-splash* of his hands entering the water.

Sophie stood up. It couldn't be more than three feet deep this near to the edge, and she wondered whether it got much deeper even in the middle. She wrung the water out of her hair, then splashed a handful of water onto her face and turned her eyes up again to the sky.

Mikael was floating on his back nearby.

"Sophie?" he said, coming upright and turning around to look at her.

"Yes?" she said, wading toward him and scrunching up

her eyes to make the water run off her eyelashes.

They stood next to each other for a moment without speaking. Then Mikael leaned over and cupped his hand very softly around the back of Sophie's head. He drew her toward him and planted a very gentle kiss on her lips, then drew back so that he could look at her.

Sophie's heart was pounding. She didn't know what to say. She had hardly any clothes on—and it was not a very flattering bathing suit, either!

Mikael seemed more frustrated than flustered.

"Sophie!" he burst out. "You must know I have been wanting to kiss you, only I promised my mother I would do no such thing while you were under our roof as a guest!"

Sophie had to laugh. It was not very romantic to have Mikael's mother brought into the conversation, but she could see why both Mikael and his mother would believe it was only honorable to leave a guest untouched.

"But, Mikael," she said, unable to keep the quaver of a smile out of her voice, "surely you are equivocating! When your mother said 'under our roof'—or whatever's the Danish equivalent—you know that really she meant the whole time I was living with you in København, not *literally* under her roof!"

"I hope you do not think I have behaved dishonorably," Mikael said.

"Oh, no, it certainly does not count as dishonorable

behavior," Sophie said gravely. For the first time in her life, she felt as though she might be speaking in a way that could be described as *flirtatious*. Honor mattered to her at least as much as it did to Mikael, and she did not want to tease him about something important, only it was irresistible!

"Perhaps it is more like the way there are special rules on board a ship, where the captain's word is law," she added, "or like how magic is supposed not to work over running water. So long as we're not on solid ground"—she lifted her feet up off the bottom, leaned back, and began treading water—"we might be in a moonlit land of faerie, where all ordinary day-time rules are suspended. . . ."

"That is something like what I thought, though mine was not so poetic," Mikael confessed, looking out over the path the moonlight seemed to mark for them along the canal. "But, Sophie, I want to be with you, be with you in the boyfriend-and-girlfriend kind of way—how ever will we manage it?"

"By waiting until we grow up?" Sophie suggested.

She couldn't help laughing again at the horrified look on his face, but in a way it was all one could say. The rigid armature of life in København and the utter straitjacket of honorable behavior made it hard to see how anything very magical could happen between them any sooner than that. "We certainly can't go sneaking around kissing behind your mother's back—it's too sordid!"

Already they could hear the quiet splash of Arne's steady

stroke heading back in their direction. Mikael was looking at Sophie in a way that gave her a warm feeling in her insides, but her hands and feet were growing cold, and she began treading water more vigorously to warm up.

"Your teeth are chattering, Sophie!" Mikael said.

Arne drew up to them and got to his feet. Shaking the water off, he suggested that they should all get out and dry off and get dressed as quickly as they could, then find a café that would serve them a hot drink.

A hot drink sounded distinctly desirable, but Sophie wondered whether they shouldn't go straight home instead. Fru Petersen might worry, mightn't she?

"I've got things to tell Sophie that I don't much want our mother to know about," Arne added, almost as though he could read her thoughts.

Nobel! It must be that Arne finally had a message from him for Sophie; Sophie's voice almost stuck in her throat, so eager were her questions, but Arne wouldn't say anything more until they were ensconced around the back table of an attractive little coffee shop with mugs of cocoa (for Sophie) and coffee (for the two brothers) topped with heaps of whipped cream and chocolate shavings.

"Sophie," Arne asked, "how much do you know about the work your father was doing for Nobel back in the early 1920s?"

"Not much," Sophie said, surprised that this should be

the first thing he would bring up. Surely there were more pressing matters, like when Sophie would meet with Nobel in person and get him to tell her things? "Really only what Mr. Nobel mentioned, that he was working on some sort of a device—and of course, since I've been at the institute, I've heard bits and pieces from Professor Bohr. . . ."

"Sophie's father," Arne told Mikael, "was an inventor of great insight, and even genius. At the time of his death in 1923—an explosion blew up his munitions factory, just over the Finnish border in Russia—Alan Hunter had devised an altogether new kind of weapon, one so powerful it promised to put paid to conventional warfare. All his research, though, had been conducted in such secrecy that when the factory exploded, there were no records of his work elsewhere. The personnel in that part of the compound were all killed, including Sophie's mother as well as her father; Sophie, who was there that day because her nanny had been called away for a family emergency that later proved spurious, was virtually the only survivor. The blast flung her out through an open window, and the worker who found her in the yard was amazed that she was largely uninjured, aside from some scrapes and bruises and a broken leg."

Until this evening, Sophie had known only the bare facts surrounding the explosion itself and her own near-miraculous survival. She had never heard anything so particular about the nanny or about the circumstances of her own preservation—how on earth had Arne learned all this?

"Have you actually spoken to people who were there?" she asked him eagerly.

"I have not," said Arne. "This information was given to me by Mr. Nobel, and there's no use asking more questions—I don't know where or how Nobel obtained it, except to say that there is a very good chance he will be in a position to give you the names and addresses of several people who can provide a significantly fuller picture of your parents' last days. Nobel's most concerned just now, though, with what happened to the plans your father was working on fifteen years ago."

"When he and I spoke over the telephone that day at Ardeer," Sophie said slowly, "Mr. Nobel said that after having believed, for many years, that the only set of plans had been destroyed in the explosion, he had recently learned of a second set of plans having survived the accident."

"Well, that's the other thing, Sophie . . . ," Arne said, his voice trailing off.

"What is it?" Sophie asked, putting down her cocoa and staring at him.

"It seems as though it may not have been an accident after all. . . ."

"Do you mean to say that someone blew up that factory *deliberately*?" Mikael asked.

"It was only when rumors quite recently surfaced of a set of plans sounding suspiciously like what Hunter—sorry, Sophie's father—was working on that Nobel sent a team of investigators to look into it," Arne said apologetically.

Mikael glowered at him, and Sophie, though she tried to school her expression, felt a surge of distress at Nobel's cavalier opportunism and Arne's seeming willingness to go along with his employer's disregard for Sophie's need to know everything she could.

"Needless to say," Arne added, "regrettable as it may be, a tragic explosion at a dynamite factory does not always raise suspicion—there was every reason at the time to think the blast the consequence of a workplace accident. One of Nobel's own brothers died in a similar explosion, you know."

"It's all right," said Sophie impatiently, "you don't have to dance around the question. Only if it really wasn't an accident, it's a pity they didn't think of it sooner; surely it is all so long ago by now that it will be impossible to get to the bottom of what happened!"

"What sort of rumors were there, though, about the missing plans," asked Mikael, digging a spoonful of cream out of his mug and giving the implement a meditative lick, "and what have you been able to learn since?"

"The first we heard of the plans actually came by way of Sophie herself," Arne said.

"Wait a minute," Sophie said slowly. "You're talking about the images that we saw on the pantelegraph machine in Edinburgh, aren't you? The ones that made you have a fit?"

Mikael looked puzzled, and Sophie realized she had never mentioned them to him, so she quickly filled him in: one day near the end of term back in Edinburgh, a mysterious incident had taken place in which a mechanical drawing had somehow been transmitted from the ether to the facsimile machine Sophie had been operating in chemistry class, to the teacher's all too evident surprise and dismay.

"That was the first harbinger—then Nobel put the word out that he would be interested in seeing further materials from that set of plans, and soon enough the arms dealers were all abuzz with it. Nobody had actually laid eyes on them, but it sounded as though the documents included details about an explosive process that could unleash exponentially more power than nitroglycerin, along with instructions for safely producing the raw materials needed and initiating the chain reaction."

"That sounds familiar," said Mikael, and Sophie gave him an inquisitive look.

"Indeed," Arne said, "and this brings me to our most recent concern. The process I've mentioned, the one in the plans, the one designed to produce an explosion more powerful than anything known to man—"

"Yes? What?" Sophie asked. Arne had the most terribly roundabout way of explaining things that she had ever heard!

"It's almost the identical process that Frisch and Meitner have just discovered—the one they were talking about this morning in the lunchroom. They've come up with the idea more or less independently, though they had read a few papers Sophie's father published as a postdoctoral student, and it was Bohr's letter earlier this week on the new reaction that led Nobel to order me to leave at once for København."

"Does that mean that Mr. Nobel doesn't need the old plans after all?" Sophie asked.

"On the contrary," Arne said grimly. "If they should fall into the wrong hands, the consequences could be literally devastating. The thought of their free circulation will be especially troubling if war is declared, as Nobel expects it to be at any moment."

It occurred to Sophie that several weeks had passed since she'd looked at a newspaper. She could understand only about a third of the Danish radio broadcasts that Mikael and his mother listened to, and somehow it was almost always the inconsequential joining-together words rather than the substantive ones.

People had been talking of war for so long now—all

of her conscious life, really—that even all the recent alarm had not quite brought it home to Sophie what profound changes might ensue if hostilities were declared. Sophie was in Denmark only as a visitor, though with the approval of the appropriate consulates and embassies; would she even be allowed to stay in the country, or might she be detained or interned as a foreign national in the event of war?

"I can only hope," Arne added, looking painfully worried, "that Professor Bohr will have the sense to keep a lid on what's going on here. It's pretty much hopeless, though—he has been rhapsodizing about these new discoveries to everyone he meets!"

"Yes," said Mikael, impatiently and with considerable sarcasm, "there's no doubt that this very idealistic notion about science being international and free to all comers in the spirit of intellectual inquiry makes it very difficult to keep things secret!"

"It is very strange," Arne said, his tone of perplexity making Sophie slightly want to laugh despite the gravity of the situation. "It will be a disaster for all of us—a disaster for the *planet*—if the Europeans are placed in a position to design and manufacture such a weapon. And yet he's not willing to keep these matters to himself! A noble internationalism, but distinctly dangerous."

* * *

14 September 1938

Dear Sophie:

I spent the weekend at my parents' place—the countryside is glorious at this time of year!—and had a very good visit from Jean and Priscilla. They're about to start at IRYLNS; they told me a most perplexing story about Miss Chatterjee having telephoned Priscilla and arranged to take the two of them out for tea, only for her to try to persuade them not to enroll in the program after all! I am pleased to report that they were not swayed by her blandishments. Good for them! You know neither of them would be much use in the army, but I feel certain they will excel at IRYLNS—can't you imagine Priscilla all beautifully dolled up in a gorgeous suit and awfully high-heeled shoes, and taking dictation like butter wouldn't melt in her mouth?

Sophie, I can't really tell from your letter, but it was very short—are you sure that you are quite happy in København? I notice that you do not say anything about that boy*, as Priscilla calls him—I suppose you must know him much better by now. I can hear you protesting, "But I do not at all think of him in that way!"—and, Sophie, I promise I will not pester you—but I hope you will introduce me to him one of these days so that I can see with my own eyes whether or not he is worthy of you! With love and all best wishes from your most grateful friend,*

Nan

Sophie winced at the word *grateful*. The basis of whatever ill-founded gratitude Nan might feel toward her was the séance in which Sophie had so memorably and horribly contacted Nan's brother, who had died some days earlier in a skirmish on the eastern front. Ever since Sophie had been in København, she had mercifully heard nothing from anyone dead—no voices, no knocks or raps, no nudges of any kind—and it could be described only as an enormous relief. She supposed that some tiny, greedy part of her had felt special to have been singled out with such an unusual and striking gift, but her larger rational self was horrified by the whole grotesque business and immensely relieved that this chapter of her life seemed to be over.

As she refolded the letter and tucked it back into the envelope, the cat Trismegistus leaped up onto the little writing desk and padded over to twine himself into Sophie's arms, pressing his muzzle against her face and purring like a windup toy. He seemed to know she needed comfort, and she rested her forehead on his fur and sighed.

Of all Sophie's wishes and regrets, perhaps the most heartfelt concerned her failure to persuade her school friends Jean and Priscilla not to enter the Institution for the Recruitment of Young Ladies for National Security. Sophie had been taken there for a visit by her great-aunt, a patroness and founder of the society, as a kind of warning, and further investigation had revealed a horror show behind the scenes: girls medicated and shocked and all-around brainwashed into subordinating their own wills and desires and personalities to the needs of Scotland's most influential men.

Sophie had believed that a change in government might allow Great-aunt Tabitha to put a stop to the depredations of IRYLNS, but in fact it had proved quite otherwise—political flip-flopping at the ministry seemed to have left IRYLNS even more deeply entrenched in the landscape. It was to Miss Chatterjee's credit that she had broken the seal of secrecy to the extent of trying to warn the girls away from the place, but of course they would not have listened to her.

Without realizing it, Sophie had been stripping little bits of paper off the edge of the envelope, and she found herself with a pile of confetti in front of her where Nan's letter had once been, with Trismegistus forgetting his dignity enough to bat at a few pieces and watch them propeller their floaty way down to the floor.

A knock came at the door, and Sophie called out, "Come in!"

She expected it would be Fru Petersen with a stack of neatly folded and sweet-smelling clothes, but in fact it was Mikael. She swept the remaining scraps of letter over the edge of the desk and into the palm of her hand, then disposed of them in the wastepaper basket. She felt extremely self-conscious around Mikael inside the flat, never more so than when he crossed the invisible barrier at the sill of her bedroom door.

Mikael looked around as though he did not quite know where to sit, then perched awkwardly on the trunk at the foot of the narrow bed. It was the trunk in which Sophie had escaped from Scotland, hidden inside the secret compartment that a magician friend of Miss Chatterjee's had used in his stage show. She had no way of returning it to him, not unless Miss Chatterjee sent a forwarding address—but hurtfully Sophie had heard nothing from her former history teacher since the day of that terrifying cross-country drive.

"Sophie," Mikael announced solemnly, "when Arne sends for you to come and visit Mr. Nobel, you have to let me come with you!"

Sophie looked at him with surprise.

"Yes, of course," she said. "At least, I assumed I would ask you to come and that you would say yes, but why make such a pronouncement of it? Do you think Arne would prefer you not to come?"

"No, not exactly," Mikael said, "but I am afraid he thinks you might be more biddable if he gets you on your own."

"Biddable?"

"Well, you are not always the best at standing up for yourself," Mikael pointed out.

Sophie couldn't explain why these words upset her so much—was it because they were true?—but she felt the tears well up in her eyes. She contemplated some savage retort, but swallowed her angry words, feeling a little sick to her stomach. Sometimes she felt almost as though Mikael wanted to cocoon her in protective silk wadding; as much as one might like the idea of being cared for by someone else, it was a surprisingly unpleasant sensation.

She sprang up out of her seat.

"Come on," she said, "let's go and see if there is anything good to eat in the lunchroom."

"Not a bad idea," Mikael said appraisingly. "This is the time of day when people sometimes bring cake, and there will certainly be biscuits, at the very least."

They let themselves out the front door of the flat and wandered down the hall to the lunchroom. Sophie's thought had indeed been happily timed, for the table held a huge box from Grandjean's Patisserie, and inside was still left at least a third of a delicious-looking and absolutely *huge* chocolate cake covered with heaps of whipped cream and cherries and lightly dusted with shaved curls of chocolate.

Sitting around the table were Bohr and Hevesy and the English theorist and refugee Paul Dirac and a rotund Austrian named Wolfgang Pauli, whom Sophie suspected of having bought the cake; he was known for his excessive love of all sorts of good things, including what Bohr euphemistically referred to as "wine, women, and song." They welcomed the young people and urged them to help themselves to cake and join the conversation, which hinged on a question Sophie had spent a great deal of time contemplating during the summer: whether there was really any such thing as a parapsychological sense.

"The very existence of wireless telegraphy and of radio," Bohr was saying, "must surely invalidate any notion that the human brain is capable of performing feats of telepathy. If I were wired for such things, why would I need to build an apparatus? I would simply tune my attention in to the sea of waves transmitted by other minds, as one might opt in or out of the conversation others are carrying on in another part of the room, and be able to hear their thoughts—or indeed to receive the same programs I might obtain on a radiogram. . . ."

"The evidence for telepathic communication is very strong," said Dirac, who was eating his cake in neat, appreciative forkfuls, each one containing a balanced proportion of cake and filling. "We have every reason to believe that a significant percentage of those who claim to have communicated with the dead are neither deluded nor fraudulent. I myself was once present at a séance in Cambridge at which the ethereal manifestations of James Clerk Maxwell and

Isaac Newton were both present, and I detected nothing in either spirit's communications that would have led me to discredit his authenticity."

Bohr's thought train was shunted by this remark into another direction.

Sophie was meanwhile skulking very low down in her seat and hoping Mikael wouldn't look in her direction: she hoped to have put speaking with the dead resolutely behind her, along with much else of life in Scotland.

"Have you ever thought of what it is that makes a ghost sinister?" Bohr asked, leaning forward with his eyes intent upon his interlocutor. "What is sinister, with a ghost, is precisely that one does *not* believe in it. If we believed in the ghost in some straightforward way, as we believe in the real physical existence of a burglar or a wild animal, it would be only *dangerous*. The fact that we do *not* believe in it—that is what changes it from dangerous to sinister. Thus the highly real phenomenon of eeriness. . . ."

Dirac was not ready to let the former matter drop.

"That is muddled thinking," he said. "You are twisting the meaning of the word *belief* beyond what it will bear. I believe in the atom, even though I will never see it with my own eyes. The atom is not sinister, but it is certainly dangerous. . . ."

"If it is possible to receive the thoughts of the dead," Bohr said irritably, "then it should also be possible to detect the thoughts of the living! Why, then, does someone not retain the services of a medium to read the thoughts of the European emperor, or perhaps the czar of Russia? It would be far more useful to know whether Europe is contemplating invading Denmark than whether Great-aunt Bertha, as it were, continues to enjoy the celestial bridge games in the elysian fields. . . ."

"For all we know," said Dirac, his manner as dry as ever (to Sophie he seemed enviably free of emotion, she still not having weaned herself altogether from the notion that the true perfection of human nature would be a calm, impassive rationality of the kind associated with the disembodied brain in a science-fiction novel), "there are a dozen mediums doing precisely that. You must allow, Bohr, that the causes of certain things are hidden from us, and may remain so."

"That, I do not dispute," said Bohr. "But as soon as we allow there to be such a thing as, say, a sixth sense, we beg the question of what constitutes that sense! I believe that the salmon, for instance, has a wonderful and deeply mysterious ability to trace a path back to the place where it was spawned. The fish is born in a mountain lake. It swims down brooks and rivers"—he took the sugar bowl and used it to weave a path around the obstacles on the table—"to the ocean. But when the time comes for the fish to reproduce, it finds its way home to the exact same pool it was born in. Does this fill me with a deep wonder as to the amazing ways of nature? Yes. Need I invoke a sixth sense? What would be the physical basis for the function of such a sense? Where is it located, and how does it work?"

Hevesy had been following the exchange with his usual look of detached, slightly ironic interest. At this juncture he leaned forward.

"The fish finds its way home," he said softly, "because the fish does not know enough to ask questions. Future investigations will likely reveal the physiological mechanism underlying the salmon's path-finding ability—but the salmon cannot apply that ability to finding, say, the best overland route—or even a route by water!—from København to Elsinore. The fish has only one task to perform—he does not choose among alternatives; he exists under the weight of a single imperative. We human beings, on the other hand, have divided the world up into choices."

Later that afternoon, Sophie lay on her bed reading a book and pleasantly digesting a large portion of cake when Fru Petersen leaned her head around the door.

"Sophie," she said in considerable agitation; Sophie had never seen her so ruffled. "Oh, Sophie! I don't suppose you especially heard the bell ringing just now—but it was the boy from the telegraph company. He has brought something truly terrible!"

"What is it?" Sophie asked stupidly, though as she looked at the yellow envelope in Fru Petersen's hand she suddenly guessed what it might be.

Fru Petersen simply gave Sophie the telegram, which was from Sophie's great-aunt Tabitha's solicitor.

> Regret announce sudden death Miss Tabitha Hunter. Details to follow—condolences to Miss Sophie Hunter—burial arrangements do not—repeat DO NOT—require younger Miss Hunter's return to Scotland, as per deceased's instructions.

Fru Petersen laid a hand on Sophie's shoulder, but Sophie shrugged it off. The older woman sat beside her for some minutes, but Sophie wouldn't even look at her. She lay facing in the other direction, stiff and unresponsive, until Fru Petersen finally brushed her hand lightly over Sophie's hair and stood up and went away.

The sound of the door closing was Sophie's cue to throw herself on the bed and begin crying. After a bout of hard, gulping sobs, she felt Trismegistus install himself along her side. She grasped him with both hands and pressed him to her chest. For once, he made no demur, resting quietly beside her as she wept, then sitting up and beginning the process (surprisingly dainty for such a thuggish-looking cat) of paw cleaning and grooming as Sophie far less elegantly blew her nose and drank a long swallow of water from the nighttime tumbler on her bedside table.

Sophie hated feeling emotions of any sort. She had a strange kind of shame at how strongly affected she was by the news of Great-aunt Tabitha's death. If only she could remain coolly unaffected by bad news, pain, and loss—if she could choose, she thought she would go and live on a desert island so as never to have to suffer the pain of losing somebody ever again! But of course it was not possible.

Her eyes felt swollen and sore, and she wished she could stay in this little room without having to talk to anyone ever again, but it was cowardly not to make herself go out and face the others. She felt unpleasantly grumpy and sad as she pushed Trismegistus off the bed and rolled her legs over onto the floor.

At school on Monday morning, the teacher must have said something to the class while Sophie was receiving condolences from the headmistress, for two very snooty girls who had hitherto hardly given Sophie the time of day invited her to sit with them at lunch, and a rather grubby but pleasant

Russian boy—a diplomat's son—offered her half his bar of chocolate.

Riding the tram home after school, Sophie was so thoroughly lost in thought that she almost failed to get off at Blegdamsvej. Only the driver's friendly reminder prevented her from riding all the way to the terminus.

She understood why it would be impossible to go to Great-aunt Tabitha's funeral. Sophie had barely gotten out of Scotland *once*—it would be tempting fate to hope to do so a second time. But the person Sophie would have given anything to see just now—the person who would be terribly pained by Sophie's absence from the funeral, since she loved the proprieties almost as much as she loved Sophie—was Tabitha's housekeeper, Peggy, who had raised Sophie from when she was very young. She must write Peggy a letter at once, Sophie resolved, and get a stamp from Fru Petersen to post it.

It was difficult to concentrate on even the easiest bits of homework. Sophie's attention kept drifting, and she felt sick to her stomach when she thought of that last brief conversation she had had with her great-aunt at Ardeer. Great-aunt Tabitha had told Sophie she must go, but Sophie still felt guilty about leaving.

After an hour and a half, Sophie had written a grand total of zero pages of her history essay, and she laid down her pen and went to the kitchen to ask Fru Petersen about postage.

The kitchen was empty, but Sophie heard voices in the sitting room. It couldn't be Mikael and his mother talking, though, could it? He had football practice after school four days a week and rarely got home until just before supper.

Fru Petersen jumped up from her seat as Sophie came into the room. Her companion, Sophie was startled to see, was Niels Bohr himself. He had never visited the flat during Sophie's stay, and she felt curious or even a little worried as to why he'd broken the unwritten law that kept him from the Petersens' apartment.

"Sophie, Professor Bohr would like a word with you," said Fru Petersen in some agitation, leaving Sophie alone with the physicist, who slouched in an armchair with his feet up on the coffee table, a large brown envelope in his hand.

"I would have been happy to come downstairs," Sophie protested, feeling distinctly unworthy of Bohr's visit.

"I thought we'd have more privacy up here than downstairs," Bohr said, sounding almost as unhappy as Sophie felt, "and Fru Petersen was kind enough to suggest we borrow her sitting room."

Sophie took a chair opposite him; Trismegistus had followed her into the room and now leaped up in several stages onto the high bookshelf perch he seemed to prefer.

"Sophie, I'm afraid I'm not here simply to offer my condolences in person," said Bohr, "though I hope you will believe me when I say that I am most heartily sorry for your loss. I met Miss Hunter several times—we were both on the program at the ISPPS conference in Estonia several summers ago, and I liked her very much—or perhaps I will say I *appreciated* her. She was far too tough a customer to merit something as ordinary as mere liking!"

Sophie muttered something, and was appalled to realize that the tears had come to her eyes again. It would be too, too awful to cry in front of Niels Bohr! She leaned down and fiddled a bit with the buckles of her school shoes to cover her confusion.

"I got a telephone call this morning from Miss Hunter's solicitor," Bohr continued. He seemed oddly reluctant to proceed, the words coming very slowly from his usually precipitous tongue.

"What did he say?" Sophie asked.

Bohr resettled himself in his chair and gave Sophie a mournful look.

"Frankly, I found it hard to believe myself," he said slowly.

"Believe what?"

"I'd have sworn she'd never—but then, my thoughts don't come into the matter. Last night, when Fru Petersen telephoned to tell me of Miss Hunter's death, I assumed it must have been a heart attack or a stroke—something of that sort."

"Was it not, then?" Sophie asked, aware that she had made exactly the same assumption as Bohr.

"I am very sorry to have to tell you this, Sophie, but Tabitha Hunter took her own life."

It was the last thing Sophie had expected him to say.

"You mean to say she committed suicide?"

It was just about possible to imagine someone else killing Great-aunt Tabitha—she had always taken pride in her willingness to stand up for unpopular causes, and many powerful people must have felt the sharp edge of her tongue over the years. But what on earth could have driven that old battle-ax to kill *herself*?

"I'm afraid so," Bohr said. "As I mentioned, I could hardly believe it myself, but I've got some supplementary evidence here that, though circumstantial, tells a story that makes some kind of sense, however grim. The solicitor assembled this packet for you—I was able to call in a favor and have it sent in the diplomatic pouch. It includes an article from the *Scotsman*—that's the only thing I've looked at, as the other materials are sealed and marked as confidential, for your eyes only. Apparently Miss Hunter read a proof copy of the article before publication and then took an overdose of a sleeping draft her doctor had prescribed for her a few months earlier. She was dead not long after midnight as Friday night led into Saturday morning, or so the coroner guesses. They'll do a full postmortem later this week."

A postmortem . . . But Sophie put aside the thought of her great-aunt's body being dissected. She took the packet that Bohr was holding out to her.

"I'll leave you to examine the contents in peace," he said. "I'll be in the office downstairs for several more hours this evening, if you'd like to talk about anything afterward, and of course you're welcome to stop by later this week.

"I've spoken with the newsagent," he added, "and we'll have the Scottish papers delivered every day until further notice—I fear we may see additional revelations in coming days, and it will be better for us to know what's going on than to depend on your family's solicitor for updates."

Sophie could only stare at him.

The word *family* grated on her ears. Sophie was the only Hunter remaining.

What on earth could be in the envelope?

Her fingers itched to slide under the flap. It seemed impolite to open it while Bohr was still present, but as soon as he had gone, she impatiently slit the fold.

When she shook the contents out onto the table, she found—in addition to the wad of newspaper that had been clipped to the outside of the envelope, presumably the article to which Bohr had alluded—two photographs, an official document sealed in Switzerland, and a fat letter in another smaller envelope, this one addressed to Miss Sophie Hunter in Great-aunt Tabitha's familiar, slightly crabbed handwriting.

She set the letter and the sealed document beside the newspaper clipping and examined the pictures first.

A young woman, not pretty but with an appealingly lively expression and thick, dark hair coiled up onto her head—it was Great-aunt Tabitha, Sophie realized with amazement, having never before seen such an attractive photograph of her great-aunt as a girl. Tabitha was wearing a well-cut and slightly masculine blouse with the sleeves rolled up to her elbows; her waist was slim, and her long, dark skirt flared out around her ankles. Clasping her arm was an older gentleman, quite dapper in his dress and wearing a straw boater. They stood on a seaside boardwalk or something of the sort—a black-and-gold stamp at the bottom of the photograph said *San Remo, 1895*. San Remo was in Italy, Sophie knew, which had not yet at that time been incorporated into the European Federation.

Though the man in the picture was surely old enough to be Tabitha's father, it was quite clear that he was no such thing—Sophie had rarely seen a picture of two people more clearly in love with each other.

Tabitha—in love?

She turned over the picture to see if anything was written on the back. Just three words: *Tabitha and Alfred.*

Sophie suddenly felt quite sick. She turned the picture over and took a closer look at the man's face, surprised that she had not recognized it at once. Now it was unmistakable. Sophie had seen tens or even hundreds of pictures of him over the years, including the likeness on the Scottish five-shilling note.

Tabitha had been in love with Alfred Nobel!

The other picture was of somewhat more recent vintage. The overriding sensation it gave Sophie was rage at her great-aunt for never having shown it to Sophie before, for it was a lovely snapshot of Sophie's parents in what must have been the very early days of their marriage. They were with another woman, sprawled out on lounge chairs of the garden-furniture variety in a forest grove—the two women had tall glasses of what might have been lemonade and wore light-colored summer dresses, while Sophie's father held a bottle of beer.

The bottle's label said BALTICA, in Cyrillic script, and Sophie guessed they must have been somewhere in the Russian countryside. But who was the other woman?

Again, on the back of the photograph, in a handwriting

that was unfamiliar to Sophie but that she guessed might have been her mother's, a legend: *Alan, Rosie, and Miss Elsa Blix,* the words read, *enjoying an uncharacteristic day of rest from their labors! August 1921.*

Elsa Blix—Sophie had never heard the name before. She must ask Professor Bohr whether the woman had been another of the cohort of postdoctoral students at the institute—might she not have been a coworker at the Russian dynamite factory where Sophie's parents had met their end, in an explosion that would occur less than two years after this picture had been taken?

Without more background information, Sophie could make little sense of either picture, so she turned next to the newspaper story, which she read with an increasing sense of disorientation and dismay.

MINISTRY ORDERS INVESTIGATION INTO SECRETIVE AGENCY. DIRECTORS FACE PROSECUTION UNDER HANSEATIC CODE OF HUMAN RIGHTS.

A police raid on the Adam Smith College in Buccleugh Place revealed a horrifying scene: dozens of young girls, many of them bearing grotesque surgical scars and suffering significant mental and physical impairments. They had entered what they thought was an elite training program for the crème de la crème of Scottish girlhood—the much-vaunted Institution for the Recruitment of Young Ladies for National Security, familiarly known as IRYLNS (pronounced "irons"). Instead they found themselves in a hell of electroshock treatments, neurochemical stimulation, and sexual abuse.

The girls of IRYLNS populate the corridors of power throughout this country, managing the offices of captains of industry and parliamentary ministers; their good looks, charming manners, and impeccable professionalism have made them some of the most sought-after female employees in the country. Meanwhile, the program's "rejects" are hidden away in an archipelago of secret hospitals and institutions, sequestered in sealed units where doctors and nurses work to conceal these damaged girls from the public eye.

The institute's director, Dr. Susan Ferrier, was not available for comment, but will be required to answer questions should the rumored parliamentary inquiry proceed. Cofounder Tabitha Hunter, former president of the Scottish Society for Psychical Research and a prominent member of Edinburgh society, issued a written statement proclaiming her

> belief that no sacrifice is too great when it comes to Scotland's security, and stating that the accusations about abuse have been much exaggerated. She said she had no regrets about her involvement in the scheme, and argued that its failures had to be put in the context of exceptional and widespread success.
>
> Further revelations will doubtless emerge in coming days, not just about the brutalities inflicted upon these innocent young girls but about the scandalous past of one of Scotland's pillars of respectability.

Was this a veiled suggestion that *Great-aunt Tabitha* had a scandalous past? It seemed nearly inconceivable, but then Sophie still couldn't understand how even this assault on her great-aunt's beloved IRYLNS could have driven Tabitha Hunter to kill herself.

She contemplated the two remaining documents. Which one to open first? She chose the slighter one, broke the seal on the outside, and found inside a notarized copy of what seemed to be a birth certificate. It was Sophie's father's birth certificate, she realized a moment later—but why should Great-aunt Tabitha have chosen to send it to Sophie now?

Then she took a second look, feeling as though the wind

had been knocked out of her.

Sophie had never known her grandparents, but she had always understood her father to be the son of one of Tabitha's first cousins. He had been orphaned at a young age, like Sophie herself—she believed his parents had died in a skiing accident—and then been taken in and raised by Great-aunt Tabitha, out of the fondness of her heart conjoined with a strong desire to ensure the survival of the Hunter line.

But the spot on the birth certificate for the father's name was blank, while the mother's was quite clearly and explicitly filled in: *Tabitha Hunter, spinster.*

Sophie's father had been Tabitha's illegitimate child!

Tabitha—a mother?

Great-aunt Tabitha hadn't been Sophie's great-aunt at all, but her grandmother!

The conclusion was inescapable. Sophie's hands seemed to act independently of her mind as they shuffled the picture of Tabitha and Alfred Nobel out of the pile. She looked at it again now with a horrid surmise.

There was no father named on the birth certificate, but it would have been very natural for the unmarried Tabitha to keep the father's name secret—indeed, she must have gone to considerable trouble to suppress the fact of having given birth to a child, for Sophie had never heard even a whisper of a stain on Tabitha's blemishless reputation. There must have been a ruthless eradication of evidence—presumably Tabitha's belief in the power of truth and her respect for the historical record had won out over the need for secrecy and respectability, but Sophie guessed it would have been a close call.

But Sophie knew her great-aunt's—her grandmother's!—way of thinking. Taken together with the birth certificate, the message of the photograph was unequivocal.

Tabitha wanted Sophie to know that Alfred Nobel was the father of her child. That meant Nobel was Sophie's grandfather.

Sophie involuntarily heaved a huge sigh. What would Tabitha spring on her in the letter?

It was almost a relief when Fru Petersen at that moment called her to supper. The letter could wait till afterward. Sophie had to force herself to swallow the chicken and dumplings she was served, and she ate her plate of stewed fruit and custard so absentmindedly that she could not even have said, once the china had been cleared, whether the fruit had been plums or apricots. Mikael wanted to play checkers, but Sophie made her excuses and returned to the bedroom, throwing herself down on the bed and removing the letter from the waistband of her skirt, where she had tucked the entire envelope of materials for safekeeping.

Friday, ten o'clock
My dear Sophie,

It is with deepest regret that I set pen to paper to wish you farewell. As a child, my heart thrilled to the heroic deeds of the ancient Romans. It seems ludicrous now, but I thought myself a sort of junior Cato or Brutus, and practiced falling on my "sword": in reality, a rake I had filched from the garden shed at Heriot Row—for as you know, Sophie, I grew up in the same house where you spent your childhood, though you should feel no obligation to keep it if it proves a millstone—the lawyers will administer the trust on your behalf, and when you are twenty-five you may decide how to dispose of the property, with the exception of my books and papers. The former, of course, will go to the library at the Society for Psychical Research, while the latter will be sealed for fifty years and placed in the archive of the National Library.

By the time you read this, I will be dead. A melodramatic pronouncement! Alas, despite that youthful admiration for Socrates and Seneca, I had not imagined I would ever be put in a position where the most attractive avenue available to me was death by my own hand. You will have read at least the initial newspaper story about IRYLNS. Susan Ferrier is determined to see things through, and believes that some remnant of the program may be salvaged. She intends to testify in support of our cherished scheme. But as the events of the past few weeks have unfolded, I have come to deem myself so great a liability that my continuing presence on the scene can only further discredit a program whose successes are everywhere evident and whose few blemishes—nay, I will use the word failures*—are now receiving undue attention from a country forgetful of what it owes to several generations of young women willing to give up their own pleasures and potential for the sake of the greater good.*

I stray from the matter of my letter! When did the habit of digression creep upon me? What you do not know, Sophie, is that one of the reporters responsible for the story about to appear in the Scotsman *has got hold of some highly incriminating information about my past, and his threat to expose it, though I would not shrink from the scandal merely on my own account, is part of a plot I will not brook! He means to halt all the progress we've made at IRYLNS, to disband the program and send all the girls home to their families, thereby depriving the country of one of its most valuable resources at a time of great—one might even say the greatest—need.*

If you have looked at the other things I enclosed for Mr. Erskine to send to your attention in København, you will not be surprised when I confess to you the deepest secret I ever kept: I gave birth to your father myself, and covered up his origins so successfully that not just the world at large but even he himself never suspected it.

The summer after I finished my undergraduate degree, I went to Italy. I have no remorse. I fell in love, I forgot myself. . . .

At the time I made the choice to cover up my transgression (as some would call it, though in truth it has always struck me as unfair how unequal the consequences should be for the man and the woman in such cases), giving birth to a child outside of marriage would have been enough to exclude me forever from circles of respectability. Alfred Nobel was already married, though he and his wife had been separated for the best part of a decade. Marriage was therefore out of the question, and I cannot honestly say that marrying Alfred would have suited my own idea of what I was meant to do in life: perhaps in the future marriage will become less restrictive, but not, I think, in our own time (and I use the pronoun our *advisedly, Sophie, for there has hardly been much change on this front over the forty-odd years I've spent working on behalf of women's equality). Ah, again I digress!*

I suppose, Sophie, this is all more difficult and unpleasant for me than I am quite comfortable saying.

I knew I was with child, and that I would need Alfred's help to conceal my condition in circumstances of reasonable comfort and propriety. He willingly settled an annuity upon me, and I took a room in a pension in Switzerland. Alfred was very sorry that I would not marry him, but as I told him, if he had wanted a divorce from his wife, he could have obtained it at any point during their separation, and I did not choose to precipitate so dramatic and necessarily public a rearrangement of his personal circumstances.

I gave birth late that spring to a baby boy—your father, Alan Hunter—and hired a wet nurse for him. I also began to fabricate a history that would later account for his presence in my life in Scotland, meanwhile returning to Edinburgh and picking up the threads of my real life.

Nobody thought twice the year after, when I became the guardian of a cousin's child, an infant boy—it was generally accepted (it is what he always believed himself) that he had been tragically orphaned in an avalanche in the Alps—and I was able to watch over Alan's education very closely, though of course he never knew that I was his mother. There was no need for him to possess a piece of information momentous enough that a child might have found it difficult to keep the secret—just as I never saw fit to tell you, Sophie, that the story about your father's adoption was a falsehood.

It was a very great blow to me when your father was killed. I hardly knew your mother, but she surely made Alan very happy, and (I believe) he her; the letters he sent in the months before his death were full of excitement about his life with the two of you, as well as about the project he was working on. I know little of that work beyond the fact that it grew out of what he had done at Bohr's institute; your mother became increasingly involved in it, too. The other person who loomed large in those letters was a slightly shadowy figure called Elsa Blix. She is the other woman in the second photograph I have enclosed—your mother spoke very highly of her, and your father seemed taken with her to a point only just this side of idolatry, but I detected some cooling off in the last few letters I ever received from him. Unlike your parents, Miss Blix was not killed in the accident, and it may be that she is the person living who can give you the fullest account of your parents' last months. You have been very good, Sophie, about not pestering me with questions I was in some instances unable but perhaps more often merely unwilling to answer; I suspect, though, that the desire to uncover more of that story may live still in your heart.

I take other secrets with me to my grave, secrets that have nothing to do with our family and that will be revealed to future historians only when the archive is unsealed. I have set the date far enough in the future that (should civilization survive so long, which is by no means a certainty should we continue on the present trajectory) such revelations as may emerge from the pages of my letters and diaries will bring down no governments.

I regret that my decision to conceal this significant chapter in my early life may have colored my subsequent dealings with those to whom I should have been closest—but I trust you will believe it to be only the truth when I subscribe myself, this one and only time, as your fond grandmother,

Tabitha Hunter

The mixture of feelings Sophie experienced in the wake of the packet's revelations could not be described. She felt betrayed; she felt vindicated; she felt illuminated; she felt mystified. She was very tempted to confide in Mikael, but she shrank (she knew it was old-fashioned) from sharing with him something that touched so explicitly on Great-aunt Tabitha's sexual past.

After a very inattentive day at school, during which she earned several reprimands, Sophie decided that there was one actual concrete puzzle she could do something about, and she went straight from the tram stop to find Bohr in his office.

Even through her preoccupied haze, Sophie caught some worrying bits of conversation as the secretary put various telephone calls through to Bohr—it sounded as though the president of Sweden and the Finnish minister of defense were both impatient to speak with him, and Sophie couldn't help but wonder whether the precarious peace between Europe and the New Hanseatic League might be now really and truly reaching its final days.

When Sophie finally got in to see him, Bohr looked even more harried than usual. He offered her a piece of a gigantic American chocolate bar that sat half-unwrapped on his desk, then asked her how she was doing.

"I don't have long, I'm afraid, Sophie," he added. "It's tricky just now—this time it really seems as though the Finns aren't going to back down. With Scotland's support and a bit of egging on from the Baltic states, they're saying that European incursions into Lithuania mustn't be allowed to continue—who knows where this will all end. . . ."

"I can come back another time," Sophie offered, sorry that her own personal troubles should impinge on Bohr's hugely more consequential geopolitical concerns.

"No, no," Bohr said, though his eye strayed to the clock.

"I will make it quick," Sophie promised. "There were all sorts of curious things in that packet, but one of the oddest was a picture of my parents with a woman called Elsa Blix."

"Elsa Blix!" Bohr said. "Yes, indeed, she overlapped with your father at the institute, and though I do not know that her contributions to the project were enormous, she was out there in Russia for most of the time your father was working for Nobel. I gathered that they had some sort of falling-out—she must have been gone for at least a month or two before the factory blew up."

"What led to their disagreement, do you remember?" Sophie asked.

"I fear it is not a question of remembering—it is something I never knew. None of us did. There were rumors, of course, and malicious gossip hinted that your mother had suspected Elsa of setting her cap at Alan and asked her to leave. I do not believe a word of it myself. Elsa was a singularly ambitious young woman, and it is far more likely that she felt her advancement there to be limited and sought greener pastures elsewhere—the woman I knew would have been unlikely to let something to do with personal relationships get in the way of her career."

"Do you know where I might find her now?" said Sophie.

"She has become quite prominent in certain circles," Bohr said thoughtfully, "though I would not say that her name is generally known. It is many years since she could be described as a pure research scientist, though she was an unusually talented experimentalist—she had the hands for it, as well as the intelligence and the imagination. She had a special interest in explosives, and though it is a reductive name for a role of some complexity, I would have to describe her now as a weapons dealer."

"A weapons dealer?" Sophie echoed. It was the last thing she had expected him to say.

"They call her the Snow Queen," said Bohr, his gaze gone somehow misty and vague. "She is rumored to have built herself a stronghold on the remote island of Spitsbergen above the Arctic Circle. If that's true, it's an extraordinary place to have chosen to put a factory; it's virtually inaccessible for whole chunks of the year, and the weather is truly wretched! On the other hand, the island itself is very rich in raw materials, with a well-developed mining industry, so I suppose she must find it worth her while."

"If I wrote her a letter," Sophie asked, "do you think she would be able to tell me anything valuable about my parents?"

"I don't know, Sophie," Bohr said gently, though Sophie thought he looked wary. "I'm not a great admirer of Miss Blix, in case you hadn't gathered. I suppose she may well know something that would be worth learning, but I'd approach the whole project of contacting her with considerable caution."

Sophie felt discouraged. In any case, it wasn't as though one could just write a letter to Elsa Blix and inscribe the word *Spitsbergen* underneath the name and expect it to reach her. But her mood brightened when Bohr added, "Let me ask a question or two to put things in motion, Sophie. Alfred Nobel will almost certainly be able to tell me how to find her. I will also see if I can learn exactly what she's up to these days—I would like us to have a little more information before we proceed."

He looked so tired as he uttered the words that Sophie was stabbed with a pang of remorse for having troubled him, and when he asked if there was anything else she wanted to talk about, she muttered a denial and rose to leave him to get back to work.

At breakfast the next morning Mikael asked his mother what they would do if war were declared.

"I have discussed it with Niels Bohr," she answered him, "and in the event of war, it may be best for you and Sophie to leave the country."

Sophie laid down her spoon. Trismegistus took note and assumed a waiting position beside Sophie's chair. He did not eat porridge, but he would lap up the milk from around the edges, with its hint of cinnamon-cardamom and brown-sugar sweetness.

"What would happen to Tris?" she asked.

"The cat will be fine, Sophie," Fru Petersen said patiently. "It's by no means certain that you'll need to travel in the first place, but if you do go, I'll take good care of him for you while you're away. You can't have him in your luggage!"

Trismegistus's hackles were rising, and it was almost as

if Sophie could actually hear the thought pass through his head: *Me—luggage?!*

"You can't expect me to leave him behind—it will be better to bring Tris than a suitcase of clothes, if I can really carry only one thing at once!"

"If he weren't so enormous, it wouldn't pose such a problem," Mikael said, assessing the cat with a look. "You'd better stop giving him porridge, Sophie! I suppose you need some easy way of moving him, perhaps a basket or a trolley. The bicycle shed is full of all sorts of old parts and tools and so forth—I'll do a bit of work on your bike tomorrow, Sophie, and it won't be any trouble at all to give you a couple of panniers and a basket at the front for the cat to ride in."

"Mikael, what kind of ideas are you putting into Sophie's head?" his mother asked, staring at him. "There is absolutely no reason to think that we would be fleeing the city with our belongings strapped to bicycles—you are painting a distinctly disturbing picture. I do not want you to give Sophie the wrong idea!"

"It's quite sensible to make sure one has an alternate means of transport in the event of evacuation," Mikael said calmly, "or so they were telling us at school assembly the other day."

Mikael's mother made a grumbling noise that spoke to

her disagreement without actually insisting on making an argument out of it.

That afternoon Sophie was doing her mathematics homework when Mikael came into the room to find her.

"Sophie?" he said.

She kept her eyes very firmly fixed on her work.

"Yes?" she said.

"I don't want to persecute you, but I thought you might want to talk about that letter from your great-aunt."

Sophie felt unaccountably annoyed, almost *savagely* annoyed. She wished she could punch him, only she was afraid that any physical contact might lead to her simply and mortifyingly melting into his arms. She felt the strangest mix of wanting to tell him everything—*everything!*—and wanting to flee his company and avoid him resolutely for the rest of her life.

"Well, if you do not want to talk about it, I will not press you," Mikael said.

Even the kindness in his voice made Sophie irrationally more furious, and she blinked to catch the tears she was afraid might spill over the lids of her eyes.

"If you do not want to talk," he said (oh, she did not deserve someone so nice as this!), "let us go and investigate the shed—at least we can get this business of the wretched cat's transportation sorted out; that will be one less thing for you to worry about."

His words were affectionate rather than chastising, but she still felt them as a reproach. Outside the shed, they found Bohr down on his knees weeding a flower bed; it was something he did for relaxation, and though it seemed an odd habit for such an important man, his secretary periodically shooed him out of the office to clear his head by working in the garden. His unlit pipe lay on a wooden seat a few feet away, a heap of dead matches beside it speaking to the usual struggle, but he picked it up again and came with Sophie and Mikael when he heard that they were contemplating adding a cat-carrying module to Sophie's bicycle.

Sophie's thoughts wandered as the other two picked through heaps of junk and exclaimed at various finds. Soon enough they had built a rig for Sophie to test, and though at first it made her feel very off balance and worry about whether she had enough side clearance given the wire baskets that had been added over either side of the rear wheel, she came to agree with the machine's improvers that it was an admirably lightweight and convenient solution.

The contraption they had fixed to the front of the bike for Trismegistus (or "that fat cat of yours," as Mikael sometimes called him) had a wood frame covered with netting and a sheepskin at the bottom so that the cat could rest comfortably.

"You'll have to shut him in, I think," Bohr observed as

he showed Sophie how the latch worked on the . . . well, if Tris were not going to be asked to get in it, Sophie might have called it a trap, it was so much like one of the pots used to catch lobsters in the Atlantic fisheries, but that was a tactless word and Sophie resolved to banish it utterly from her thoughts. The *receptacle*—that was a good, dignified term.

It was nice to have a bicycle evacuation system, but it would be even better not to need it.

During the week that followed, Sophie was unusually aware of the miasma of metaphysics that seemed to permeate the whole city of København. Bohr's musings on how light could be a wave and a particle at the same time had recently caused one pragmatic French visitor to observe that the Danish physicist's thinking was shrouded in the mists of the north, and though København was actually no farther north than Edinburgh (the two cities were at virtually the same latitude), the Hanseatic identity of Denmark was much more pronounced than anything Sophie had ever encountered in Scotland.

She supposed there was no reason physics could not be practiced in southern climes, but sometimes she wondered whether the science itself was not thoroughly and inextricably bound up with the idea of north. She took a strange national pride in the fact that one of the great innovators in physics was a Scot, Charles Thomson Rees Wilson. He had built the first cloud chamber in 1911 at the famous laboratory in Cambridge, coming subsequently to be known as "Cloud" Wilson: a comical but romantic name. A cloud chamber made invisible things visible, with tracks of particles like squiggly glowworms caught writhing their way across the photographic paper. The idea for the invention had come to Wilson during the time he had spent in the observatory on Ben Nevis, the highest mountain in Scotland, looking at the optical phenomena of sun shining on clouds surrounding hilltops: coronas, colored rings, the shadows on mist or cloud called *glory*.

All that week Bohr was consuming vast quantities of chocolate—one afternoon his secretary actually sent Sophie back out twice to the corner shop for additional supplies—and the only reason he did not get through an even more implausibly huge supply of tobacco was that he had such a habit of letting his pipe go out, then asking helplessly, after trying and failing to get a draw on it and feeling uselessly in all his pockets, "Do you perhaps have a match?"

Sophie's assistance was not limited to the purchase of sweets. She was enlisted to help in the office with supplementary typing, and was very glad now of having learned all those tiresome office skills at school in Edinburgh, as they offered the only small way in which she might contribute to the joint enterprise.

Excitement about Bohr's latest thoughts concerning the atomic nucleus ran at such heights that work on matters unrelated to the splitting of the atom had virtually ceased: if it did not involve fission, nobody was interested, though Hevesy continued to toil away with his animals in the basement. (Trismegistus would no longer go anywhere near that part of the building.) Everyone else, though, seemed to be devising experiments to test the Frisch-Meitner hypothesis or covering one blackboard after another with intriguing but deeply mysterious strings of figures.

Sophie asked Bohr once or twice about whether he'd obtained any more information about Elsa Blix and her current activities and whereabouts, but his thoughts were thoroughly elsewhere, and the most she could gather was that he had made several telephone calls and mentioned the name to Nobel.

Because of the current European situation, and as a particular consequence of the new racial laws that had expelled Jews from university positions in Germany, Italy, and France, all sorts of formerly far-flung colleagues had landed up at the institute, which was clearly felt to be one of the few redeeming features of what were otherwise largely stories of displacement and loss. The chance to converse with someone in person was perceived to be so valuable that Bohr himself had been known to take a long train trip solely in order to have several hours of train-station rendezvous with some particularly stimulating colleague in Oslo or Hamburg, and those whose routes might be jigged to pass through København Central Station would telephone to see if Bohr could come to the station for coffee and conversation between legs of a journey. Not just Bohr but almost everyone else at the institute seemed to believe there to be a sort of alchemy in real actual face-to-face conversation. Indeed, many of the people there, rather than doing what an outside observer could have identified as real work, spent a great deal of their time sitting around doing what Sophie's old nurse Peggy would have scathingly called *blethering.*

On Thursday of that week the legendary Wittgenstein, whose brilliance and oddity continued to be much discussed at the institute even several years after his departure, was due to pass through København. Best known as the inventor of the uncertainty principle, Wittgenstein had been befriended by Bohr when they were both studying at Manchester before the war, and as the Petersens' longtime lodger he was well-known to Mikael and his mother. (When Sophie asked Mikael what Wittgenstein was *like,* though, all Mikael could say was that he had an annoying habit of running himself a bath in the middle of the night.)

Mikael was deputized to drive Bohr to the station for the meeting. Mikael had finally got his driver's license, after a somewhat checkered career as a learner, while Bohr preferred not to drive at night ever since an accident in which one of his sons had knocked a child off her bicycle. He cycled to work every morning from the Carlsberg mansion, and rode home again as well unless the weather was exceptionally inclement. He was still much teased for his habit, while driving a car, of slowing down at a green light and speeding up at a red one, due to a cyclist's sense of how to respond to one's distance from a light about to change colors.

They drove to the station in silence, Bohr seemingly lost in thought and Sophie and Mikael reluctant to disturb him. They parked on the street near the station and walked the rest of the way. It was curious how similar it felt to the area around the central train station in Edinburgh—Sophie supposed that some set of topographical and architectural constraints must contribute to the uncanny resemblance, but it almost gave one a strange occult theory of things developing along more or less independent paths that were yet somehow entangled with one another.

She and Mikael both went into the station with Bohr

to wait for Wittgenstein's train, which had been slightly delayed. When the lanky physicist finally appeared, Mikael greeted him warmly and pressed into his hands a packet of fine cambric handkerchiefs, a present from Mikael's mother, who had suffered a great deal from the laundry-related implications of her delicate former lodger's vulnerability to hay fever and bronchitis. Wittgenstein unwrapped them and tested one out by blowing his nose, then solemnly informed Mikael that they would do.

As the two men looked about for the best place to talk (there was not much choice; it was either the station buffet or the station bar), Bohr's eye fell on Sophie and Mikael.

"Will you two be off back to the institute now?" he asked. "It will be terribly dull for you just hanging around waiting for me!"

Mikael looked at Sophie, who knew he had promised to make sure Bohr got home safely. Equally, though, they would not want to intrude on his conversation with Wittgenstein, who was already beginning to mutter something incomprehensible about radio tubes.

"It seems a pity not to take advantage of having permission to be out on a school night by *staying* out," Sophie finally said. She could not think of anything better to say, but it seemed to make sense to Bohr.

"Yes," said Mikael. "In fact, if you don't mind, it might

be that there's enough time for me to take Sophie on a quick visit to the Tivoli Gardens! And then we will be able to drive you home afterward—I know you do not like fuss, but my mother will be very annoyed if we have not actually seen you to your doorstep."

"Yes, yes, that will be an admirable way of managing things," Bohr said, his face lighting up. "You will go to the gardens! They will very soon be closed for the season—*carpe diem*!"

He consulted his watch, then took several bills from his wallet and pressed them into Mikael's palm. "Meet me back here at half past ten, perhaps?"

"I'll say!" Mikael exclaimed.

As they walked the short distance from the station, Mikael rhapsodized about København's most famous attraction.

"Sophie, you'll love the Tivoli Gardens," he said earnestly. "They're far better than anything you'll have seen in Scotland. They were laid out about a hundred years ago, with a grand fun fair modeled on the famous ones in Paris and New York, in order to distract everyone from the awfulness of what was going on in politics—it worked then, and it works now!"

By this time they were well out of earshot of the physicists, and Sophie could not resist asking a question that had been weighing on her mind.

"What do you think Mr. Wittgenstein would have done," she said, "if he hadn't found those handkerchiefs soft enough?"

Mikael started laughing.

"He'd have given them right back to me! My mother looked for a long time to find the ones she knows he likes—they had a terrible argument right when he first arrived about the laundry having overstarched his handkerchiefs. He said that starch irritated his nasal membranes, and my mother said something unprintable!"

"Yes, I'm sure she did," Sophie said. "Mikael, do you think it's all right for us to go off and enjoy ourselves when we promised your mother we'd look after the professor?"

"She knows it's a difficult proposition to stay close by him the whole time, and she trusts us to do what's needed. He'll be fine as long as he's with Wittgenstein, and we'll make sure to be back well before Wittgenstein's due to leave."

"What is it that she's afraid will happen to him if he's left alone?" Sophie asked timidly. "Not . . . ?"

Her voice trailed off. It was the sort of thing one preferred not to put into words, but the melancholic exhaustion that was known to strike Bohr regularly had seemed intense enough recently that she couldn't help wondering if he, like

Tabitha Hunter, sometimes harbored thoughts of doing away with himself.

"Nothing so awful as suicide," Mikael said thoughtfully. He knew, of course, that Sophie's guardian's death had been declared a suicide; it was all over the Scottish papers. Otherwise Sophie had still not brought herself to take Mikael into her confidence, a failure of courage for which she frequently reproached herself. "It's just that he gets so gloomy and oppressed when he works too hard. I've seen him much worse than this, though, believe it or not."

When they were first built, the Tivoli Gardens had been just outside the walls of the original fortified city of København, but the town had expanded to such an extent that the park was now nestled right in the heart of the city. Sophie and Mikael paid their entrance fees at the ornate gates and walked through into what seemed almost like another world. The walks were tree-lined, with restaurants and cafés dotted here and there; there were bandstands and grottoes and decorative ponds, everything illuminated with electric lightbulbs so that it seemed almost as bright as day.

Sophie and Mikael wandered around an artificial lake and gasped at an illuminated pagoda-type palace, a grand pavilion like something from a picture book. As they came toward the bandstand, a smiling girl dressed in a top hat and a dinner jacket and a very short skirt indeed accosted them and urged them to see the show.

"Is there a separate charge for admission?" Mikael asked.

"Yes, but it is only two kroner."

"For one of us, or for both?" said Mikael suspiciously.

"For each of you," the girl allowed.

They were talking in Danish, and Sophie was pleased to find she could understand them, though admittedly it was the kind of simpleminded conversation that featured disproportionately in the pages of elementary language textbooks.

"What is the show?" she asked carefully.

"An astonishing display of the powers of the human mind," the girl said, "by the distinguished mentalist Hermes Trismegistus!"

Mikael's expression of disgust was so pronounced that Sophie had to choke back her laughter.

"Do let's go and see it, Mikael!" she said, taking the change purse from her pocket and beginning to look through for the right coins. "We can tell Tris when we get home that we saw his namesake!"

Mikael put his hand on hers and made her reclasp her purse.

"I'll pay, Sophie," he said grandly.

He gave the girl a bill in exchange for two tickets and

some change, and they made haste to enter the stands, as the show was about to start, and sat down near the back. The audience seemed to be made up of equal parts courting couples and families with small- to medium-size children. Sophie felt awkwardly in between stages, and wished (as she often did) that she looked more grown-up.

A cigarette girl was circulating up and down the aisles, and Mikael bought them ice cream to eat while they waited. It was a delicious slice of vanilla ice cream coated in a thin chocolate shell and wrapped in silver paper that, if one used the appropriate technique, could be folded back in stages while keeping one's fingers perfectly clean, leaving one with a neat, compact rectangle of foil at the end.

It was not long before Hermes Trismegistus appeared onstage. He looked very much as one might have expected: a stout but imposing figure in evening dress, dark hair brilliantined to reveal a significantly receded hairline, the requisite carnation in his buttonhole. His lovely assistant Lilly—a different girl from the one outside—wore a white floor-length velvet dress and had her hair up in an elegant manner that Sophie associated, though she couldn't have sworn to its being the dictionary definition, with the word *chignon*.

The opening routine did not entirely hold Sophie's attention, as she was too busy wondering about what sort of facilities were required for housing and transporting the half a dozen white doves featured.

The next bird the mentalist brought out was an altogether more impressive specimen, a parrot of some sort with a hoarse voice and a surprisingly large wingspan. Hermes Trismegistus asked a fellow a few rows ahead of Sophie and Mikael to stand up and hold a ten-kroner note at arm's length, and the parrot left his perch on the magician's knuckles and flew directly to the man with the banknote. He took the note carefully in his beak and flew back to the magician onstage, who made a great show of taking out his wallet and putting the note into it before relenting and sending the money back—by bird!—to the fellow in the audience, who was pretending to be a good sport about it but looked immensely relieved at the return of his money.

"This isn't bad," Mikael whispered to Sophie, "but I thought he was billing himself as a mentalist! This is just an ordinary magic show with trained animals. . . ."

"Let us wait and see what he does next," Sophie suggested, and indeed the next thing the magician did was to get a few people up onstage and ask each of them two or three questions before guessing their birthdays—evidently correctly, judging by the look of amazement on each participant's face, and by the questioning or reproachful glances they directed at their companions once they returned to their seats.

Mikael assured Sophie that this trick could be accomplished by way of a simple algorithm, and she believed him—yet it was hard not to be slightly awed by the performer's showmanship and by the collective gasps of an appreciative audience.

The strangest thing happened next. Sophie did not attribute psychic powers to Hermes Trismegistus—his show was almost certainly made up of different bits and pieces of trickery attractively combined and packaged, and she was determined to enjoy it for what it was. But she had to credit him with an amazing ability to read an audience, because the following bit involved his lovely assistant being blindfolded securely enough that there could be no suspicion whatsoever, even in the heart of the most inveterate skeptic, that she could receive any visual cues from the mentalist himself—and the person he called up onstage to perform the blindfolding and satisfy the skeptics was Mikael!

Together, Mikael and the mentalist went through a slightly comical pantomime that was admirably readable even from the very back of the amphitheater. The mentalist took out from his seemingly inexhaustible pockets a number of different strips of cloth—first a light-colored gauzy-looking one that Mikael indignantly rejected as too diaphanous, then a strip of gray felt that met with his grudging approval, and after that an old-fashioned blindfold made by rolling up a black silk square into a tight band. Under the magician's supervision, Mikael fixed each one in turn over the assistant's eyes, until the upper part of her face was entirely swathed in cloth.

Mikael was growing noticeably restless and irritable, but this was all part of the entertainment, as far as the audience was concerned. Laughter broke out each time he tried to leave the stage and had his hand tugged back by the magician, who finally drew from his pocket an ample black hood and made Mikael try it on.

"Does any light penetrate this barrier?" the magician asked.

Mikael shook his head.

"Can you see anything at all?" the mentalist persisted.

"Nothing whatsoever," said Mikael, his voice slightly muffled by the hood, but not so much that one could not understand what he was saying.

The magician plucked the hood from Mikael's head, then handed it back to him so that he could put it on the assistant himself. He had been very careful throughout to make sure that only Mikael secured the materials about the young lady's head. She was seated on a stool, and the magician spun her around upon it now until she came to rest with her back facing the audience.

"The technique that I am about to demonstrate," he

announced, "was once the exclusive preserve of a coterie of Buddhist monks living and studying in a monastery in remotest Tibet. Their isolation gave them unimaginable freedom from any notion of the mind's having limits, and they learned over the years to transcend the confines of the body in the most extraordinary ways."

Mikael had made his way up the steps by now and rejoined Sophie. Meanwhile the strains of the small orchestra in the pit became vaguely Eastern, with some plangent, unfamiliar melody emerging on an oboe, accompanied by a soft drumming and the high-pitched throb of bells and cymbals.

Mikael snorted.

"The mysterious East!" he whispered contemptuously to Sophie.

She kicked him to keep him quiet.

"On my own journey of spiritual inquiry—"

Mikael was groaning, but Sophie did not bother trying to shut him up this time—she was thoroughly enjoying the magician's implausible but vivid recycling of the clichés of Eastern enlightenment.

"—I found myself on the doorstep of the lamasery. I presented myself as a searcher and a seeker, a man of some spiritual acuity who little dreamed of the secrets to which I would become privy within those walls. . . ."

He proceeded to describe the monastery routine: rising

before dawn for hours of prayer, participating in a series of physical and mental exercises of exceptional stringency whose particulars he was forbidden to disclose on pain of death. (It was not clear how the sentence would be executed, but as an enthusiastic sometime reader of the popular fiction of the late nineteenth century, virtually the only light reading to be found on the shelves of the library in Heriot Row, Sophie had a vaguely Orientalist notion of opium-smoking thug assassins dispatched to do the bidding of villainous potentates.)

The upshot, the mentalist continued, was that he had learned—there was no occult component, just the sustained practice of spiritual discipline and the repetition of mental exercises, and in fact anyone who aspired to acquire such skills could purchase his small pamphlet setting forth a program for transforming a mental weakling into a veritable Hercules of the mind—how to transmit a vivid mental picture of anything he saw to another person.

"No trickery," he said solemnly. "The feat I am about to perform is nothing more or less than a testament to the amazing powers of the human mind!"

"When is he going to start the actual trick?" Mikael muttered under his breath.

"I believe he's about to," Sophie whispered. "He has to build up the suspense first, I think, or else there won't seem to be nearly enough to it. That's what the blindfold business is all about—this way he's giving people their money's worth."

"Lilly!" the mentalist called out.

"Yes?" she responded.

Her voice could be heard quite clearly despite the layers of cloth covering her face.

"Lilly, on your oath, can you see the slightest thing?" he asked.

"Not the slightest thing," she said.

"Nothing at all?"

"Nothing!"

"Not the least little peep of light?"

"Not the least little peep!"

"So that when I ask this lady"—he reached out his hand to a thoroughly respectable-looking middle-aged Danish lady, who let him raise her to her feet; she looked flustered but flattered, hitching her handbag up under her arm for fortitude—"when I ask her to hold up some object she has about her person, so that I can see it and the members of the audience can also see what it is, will you swear by the mysteries of the Egyptian pyramids and the sacred temple at Eleusis—"

Mikael snickered, and Sophie could feel, forming in her cheek, the dimple that preceded laughter.

"—that you can see nothing whatsoever?"

"Nothing whatsoever," said Lilly the assistant.

"Madam," the magician said to the lady next to him, "pray choose something you have about you and reveal it to us."

The lady unclasped a bracelet from her wrist and gave it to the magician, who held it up and placed his finger on his lips. He gave it back to the lady, then called out, "Lilly!"

Lilly's voice assumed a strange tranquillity as she began speaking.

"A silver bracelet, very pretty, with a band of red-and-blue enamelwork around it—is it birds or flowers? I can't quite see—flowers, I think, though. . . ."

Of course, the bracelet was too small and too far away for Sophie and Mikael to be able to discern all of its particulars, but it was clear from the response of those in the immediate vicinity of the bracelet's owner that Lilly had described the piece of jewelry to a T.

Hermes Trismegistus proceeded to repeat the same feat with a young man's engraved cigarette lighter and then an older gentleman's mustache clippers. "A real stumper, that!" Mikael said sardonically into Sophie's ear, and she had a difficult time not laughing out loud—gosh, it was awfully unsanitary, someone carrying such a thing around in his pocket, or using it in public!

After several more feats of mentalism—Mikael thought

the audience members must be plants, but Sophie wasn't so sure; wasn't it genuinely possible that Hermes Trismegistus had learned how to open a quite focused channel of mental communication with his partner in the act?—Hermes Trismegistus unwrapped his lovely assistant and asked the audience to give her a round of applause. He took a few bows himself. Then the lights went out.

When they came back on, both he and his assistant had vanished, and the park's ushers were quietly but effectively shepherding everyone out of the theater.

Mikael checked his watch, and whistled when he saw the time.

"Good thing that piece of charlatanry didn't last any longer! Sophie, let's make tracks; we're due back at the station in fifteen minutes. . . ."

They picked their way through the crowds and out of the park, Sophie looking regretfully at various wonders she had not had the chance to examine properly and making herself a promise to come back one day and see everything in a more leisurely manner.

Inevitably when they got back to the station Bohr wasn't at all ready to leave yet. Wittgenstein's train had been delayed by an hour, and the two men had laid out an extraordinarily complex map of condiments and cutlery and napkins to represent the nuclear reactions with which they were concerned.

Sophie and Mikael found a bench to sit on while they waited. Their attention was arrested shortly thereafter, though, by the sight of a couple in heated argument. The fact of the man and woman's both being dressed in street clothes and carrying perfectly ordinary-looking luggage could not obscure that they were the mentalist Hermes Trismegistus and his assistant Lilly.

The mentalist looked more or less as debonair and relaxed as he had onstage, but Lilly's body was gathered up into an angry, self-contained rod of fury.

They came to rest in a spot not very far from Sophie and Mikael's bench, and it was all too easy to hear what they were saying. They were speaking in English; indeed, Sophie could have sworn they both had Scottish accents (her Danish was certainly not yet good enough to identify a foreign accent in Danish).

"You're impossible, Sean," the woman was saying. "I don't know whether you've come to believe all that mystical guff you spout during the show—"

"It's not guff!" the mentalist interjected, sounding genuinely injured. "Lilly, you know that—"

"The only thing I know," she snapped, "is that you seem quite incapable of understanding what *I'm* thinking!"

"You're being unfair," said the mentalist. "If you don't tell me what you want, how am I supposed to intuit it?"

"You're the thought reader, not me!" she shouted.

"Such skills of which I am possessed," he said, "do not enable me to disentangle the confused jumble of desires and fears making up the average female psyche. . . ."

"Ouch!" Mikael whispered to Sophie. They were both mesmerized by the exchange, which had become loud enough that others in the station had begun to attend to it also.

"If you knew what you wanted, Lilly," the mentalist added portentously, "I might be able to help you to it. As it is, my hands are tied."

"I do know what I want!" Lilly said.

"What do you want?"

"I want you to want to marry me!" she shouted, and then burst into tears.

The mentalist put his arm around her and whisked a beautiful and gleamingly white silk handkerchief out of his pocket, but it was painfully obvious what he did not say.

At this juncture Bohr and Wittgenstein emerged from the buffet and began moving in Mikael and Sophie's direction. Their path took them quite close by the theatrical couple; Lilly's head was buried in the mentalist's breast, but Sophie saw the mentalist himself do a small double take when he saw Bohr.

Of course, Bohr was very celebrated, so it was hardly surprising that he should be often recognized. But as the magician followed the scientists with his eyes, he did a quite evident *second* double take when his gaze fell on Mikael and Sophie.

Had he recognized them from the show earlier?

Some large proportion of the Tivoli audience, though, must have passed through the train station afterward; the two locations were just across the road from each other, and the train was by far the most obvious way to get home after an evening out. It certainly did not explain the way that the mentalist's arm had dropped away from Lilly's shoulders as he looked back and forth between Bohr and Sophie, a speculative gleam lighting his eyes. . . .

Wittgenstein was grumbling about not having a detective story to read on the train and seemed unable to concentrate on anything Bohr was saying. He barely responded to Bohr's warm farewell, and went off to his train with nary a backward glance.

"I hope you had a good conversation with Wittgenstein, Professor Bohr," Mikael said mischievously.

"Yes, yes, most productive," Bohr said. "Mikael, I don't suppose you can identify this gentleman who is making his way toward us, can you?"

"I don't know him personally," Mikael said, surprised, "but Sophie and I saw his show just now at the Tivoli Gardens, and I can tell you that he is a self-described mentalist who performs under the name Hermes Trismegistus."

"Hermes Trismegistus?" Bohr said, his attention distracted for a moment despite the imminence of the mentalist's arrival. "Delightful! When I was a boy, I once came across an old book of alchemical texts—I spent an entire term convinced that I might discover the technique for transmuting lead into gold! Lead, of course, is a beautiful element in its own right, with quite magical properties. Let us see what this fellow wants, but if he detains us too long, Mikael, you must help me detach myself. . . ."

The mentalist was by now hard upon them. Sophie half expected him to greet Bohr with a showy low bow, but he shook hands in a fashion that even Great-aunt Tabitha might have deemed reasonably couth.

"Sean Kelly, at your service," he said.

"My name is Niels Bohr," the Danish scientist said politely, even though the other man obviously already knew who he was. "This is Mikael Petersen, and the young lady is Sophie Hunter."

"Sophie Hunter!" Kelly exclaimed, the Hermes Trismegistus self flickering showily in and out of his manner as he spoke. "Indeed, I thought it must be so—I never forget a face. I saw a photograph of the young lady earlier this year; her features stayed with me."

"What do you want?" Bohr asked, his voice neutral, but

he was usually so warm that even neutrality felt to Sophie like a kind of hostility toward the interloper.

"I feel certain the three of you will find this odd—you do not know me from Adam, as they say—but I have taken the liberty of introducing myself, at this inconveniently late hour and in a public place where Professor Bohr would doubtless prefer to pass unmolested, though it be by one of his most devoted admirers—"

Bohr looked at his watch, and the mentalist caught himself up short.

"I will cut to the chase," he said. "I believe myself to be in possession of some information that may prove interesting to Miss Hunter."

Bohr looked puzzled, and Mikael had already interposed himself physically between Sophie and the mentalist.

"Sophie," Mikael said, glaring at the performer, "tell me if you want me to make this fellow go away!"

Instead Sophie stepped forward. In her boldest voice, though she could hear it shaking a little, she asked, "What sort of information?"

"You might rather ask, information concerning what?" the mentalist said, the staginess very strongly peppering his manner.

"What, then?" Mikael asked irritably.

"It is something I heard from a woman we both knew—the

woman who had Sophie's picture and named her for me."

Suddenly Sophie knew what he would say next.

"You must be talking about Mrs. Tansy!" she exclaimed. "She called her cat after you—I wondered earlier, but now I'm sure of it. Was she terribly impressed with your stage name?"

"Strict honesty compels me to admit," said the mentalist—and it really did seem to pain him to say the words—"that the cat had the name first."

Sophie tried to keep her face grave, but she could not quite maintain her expression, and the mentalist coughed.

"I consider myself honored, I might add, to share the denomination with so distinguished a member of the species worshiped by the ancient Egyptians."

Mikael did not actually say, "Stuff it!" but his thought was almost as clear to Sophie as if he had spoken the words.

"I knew Mrs. Tansy for many years," the mentalist continued. "We worked together a few times, and I saw her not long before she died. She told me she had a commission, from a reclusive dynamiteur whose name I need not sully by airing it in public, to get the young girl in the picture out of Scotland. She was more discreet about what was supposed to happen after that, but I feel certain the sight of you here—and in such distinguished company!—would have given her considerable satisfaction."

"Why are you telling Sophie all this?" Mikael interrupted. "I don't believe Mrs. Tansy wished Sophie well—not in any straightforward sense, or at least not other than insofar as it might have brought her some kind of material benefit. I wonder whether there isn't something in it for you now, too. . . ."

"I swear by the sacred wheel of the Tibetan cosmology," the mentalist said solemnly, "that I am not in the least motivated by pecuniary considerations, but only by a disinterested desire to pay respects to a friend's memory and perhaps further the cause of good in the world, though my mentors at the monastery were continually cautioning me that any action, however well-intentioned, may initiate undesirable consequences. Is inaction on such grounds, though, perhaps overly scrupulous?"

"Get on with it, man!" Mikael snapped. "What do you have to say to Sophie?"

"You are surely fully apprised of the important part our friend the dynamiteur has played in this business," the mentalist said. "Now, *there* is a man who worships, whether he understands it or not, at the altar of Shiva, destroyer of worlds. . . ."

Bohr flinched slightly at the name Shiva, and Sophie wondered whether it didn't mean something to him.

"But Eugenia Tansy, though she was not above taking money in order, as it were, to tip the hands of the spirits one way or another, was also a woman of genuine and uncanny perceptiveness. She had a very special receptivity to goings-on in the ethereal world. And insofar as she had made a commitment to help the eminent gentleman whose name we will not contaminate by uttering it in a profane hall of locomotion—"

Mikael jabbed Sophie in the ribs. "Profane hall of locomotion?" he whispered scornfully. "A mighty fancy way of talking about a train station—mighty foolish, too! Sophie, this fellow is simply too awful; make him get to the point, can't you? See how tired Bohr looks."

Their restiveness seemed to register with the mentalist, who reined himself in and finally got to the point.

"In short, Sophie," he said, "Mrs. Tansy was concerned about possible interference by another person—a third party who had some concern in the original transactions between the dynamiteur and your father—a person who felt thwarted by the stipulations of the original agreement, and who responded to it in the most intemperate, indeed, dare I say *lethal* manner."

Even the convoluted idiom could not conceal his meaning.

"Are you saying," Sophie asked slowly, "that someone else was the loser in that original arrangement—someone who perhaps wanted to buy my father's invention, and was beaten out by—"

"Don't say the name, Sophie!" Mikael interjected, looking

around to see that nobody was listening.

"And that this person may have caused the explosion at my father's factory," Sophie continued, "in retribution for my father's not being willing to sell the device to any comer?"

"It may well be so, Sophie," said the mentalist. "At any rate, that is very much what Mrs. Tansy understood to have happened. She believed that the person in question would harbor some malevolence toward you, should he or she learn of your existence. She was highly concerned. . . ."

"Who was the person, though?" Sophie asked urgently. "If I know, I can watch out for him!"

"Alas, she did not know," the mentalist said. "If she had, she might have told the dynamiteur—he would have paid well. But the person's identity was almost fully hidden from her, which suggests to me the possibility of his or her possessing occult powers. The only thing she had to say, though I am not sure what good the information will do you, is that the color white may pose a special danger, and that you should avoid bees. . . ."

"Bees?" Sophie said. "It's an odd sort of a warning."

"Odd, and not particularly helpful," Kelly admitted, "but there it is, Sophie. As soon as I realized who you were, I knew that it was my karmic obligation to transmit this information, and I hope you will forgive me for detaining you so long. I have a train to catch myself!"

And he rejoined his assistant, who had been waiting with considerable impatience, and they and their luggage vanished permanently from this story. Sophie sometimes wondered if she would see him again, but she never did, though once or twice she spotted an old handbill half plastered over on a hoarding with the name Trismegistus just visible, and many years later she read in the newspaper that a man called Sean Kelly had been appointed curator of Tibetan manuscripts at one of the great Asian libraries.

Bohr seemed bewildered by the exchange he had just witnessed. As they walked to the car, he asked Mikael an almost comically precise series of questions, most of which Mikael could not answer.

"Of course, he can't really be capable of transmitting the object's image to his assistant," Bohr observed as Mikael unlocked the car.

"Why not, though?" Sophie asked, climbing into the backseat. "Couldn't thought be transmitted on invisible waves, like radio, and we just don't yet have the instruments to detect it?"

"It is a false analogy," Bohr said. "Forty or fifty years ago, yes, I'll give you that it still seemed a genuine possibility. But we are now living in the world of the invisible. We would be able to detect *something*—the fact that we cannot do so mitigates strongly against it, though telepathic communication between human beings seems to me at least minimally more probable than, say, the ability to see the future or to move objects by the power of the mind alone."

Sophie shifted slightly in her seat, feeling guilty at having kept from him her own confusing and contradictory mass of experiences around clairvoyance, spiritualism, and all the rest of the uncanny apparatus of her otherwise straitlaced Scottish upbringing. She herself had believed for many years that the whole thing was complete bunk, until she began hearing the voices of the dead. Those experiences had receded into the back of her consciousness during this Danish sojourn, and now seemed almost as unlikely as the childhood conviction, based on dreams, that one can actually float effortlessly along the ground without one's feet touching.

"If you'd seen the show, though, Professor," Mikael said earnestly, "you'd be racking your brains right now to work out how he pulled it off. It can't have been that he chose objects in a prearranged order—I'd swear there was no collusion with audience members. And though it's a common trick for these people to have a code, let's say an agreed-upon set of letters whereby if the speaker's sentence begins with a word whose first letter is *S*, the person wearing the blindfold guesses *scarf* or *shoe* based on some private arrangement, I am fairly certain that he wasn't feeding her enough words to make that sort of thing possible."

"Yes," Sophie interjected, "I thought he was very careful at that point to reduce the patter, just so he couldn't be suspected of communicating information to her on the sly by what he said. It is difficult to see how it would be worth his while to plant quite so many people in the audience. But, Mikael, how do you think he could have done it?"

"Ventriloquism?" Bohr suggested, sounding lively and interested. The topic had fully engaged his attention, seemingly erasing much of his fatigue.

"What do you mean?" Sophie asked.

"Am I using the right English word, Mikael?" Bohr asked.

"Yes, if you mean throwing the voice so that it appears to come from some other person or object," said Mikael. "Do you really think that might have been it?"

"In fact, the blindfold and the face coverings would make it easy," Sophie said slowly. "You wouldn't need to match the words so closely to the movement of the other person's lips."

"When I was a boy," Bohr said with enthusiasm, "I had a wonderful set of encyclopedias called *The Books of Knowledge*. There was an entry on the religion of ancient Egypt that for some reason particularly captivated me, and one of the most striking observations was that the Egyptian priests made images of the gods speak by means of ventriloquism."

"But how could we test the hypothesis?" Sophie asked.

"Does it really matter, Sophie?" Mikael said. "Surely we're dancing around the question—how on earth can that fellow have had a message for you from the wretched Mrs. Tansy?"

Guessing Bohr's likely puzzlement, Sophie leaned forward into the space between the seats in the front and briefly filled him in: how she had met the spiritualist medium at a Friday-evening séance in Heriot Row, that Mrs. Tansy had given Sophie a strange message that later turned out to have originated with Alfred Nobel himself—but that the medium had been murdered shortly afterward by someone playing a bit part in an intricate plot involving government manipulation of the perceived threat of European war.

"I knew, of course, that Nobel took an interest in you, Sophie," Bohr said pensively.

Mikael steered carefully around a corner and slowed again to allow a small marmalade cat to finish crossing the road.

"I am slightly alarmed, however," he added, "to learn that assorted charlatans throughout the Hanseatic states have been apprised of the arrangement also! Why, oh, why must Nobel encourage these rogues?"

"I don't like it much myself," Sophie admitted.

"Could either of you make any sense of the so-called

warning the fellow issued?" Bohr asked.

Mikael and Sophie confessed their joint incomprehension.

"Rather worrying for you, Sophie," Bohr said.

They had reached the mansion, and pulled up in front to let him out.

"Let me know if you have any other encounters like this, won't you, Sophie?" Bohr said as he got out, Sophie moving to the front seat to keep Mikael company for the rest of the ride home. "And, Mikael, I know I can count on you to keep an eye out. Nothing's too minor to be worth mentioning—in fact, we should all be on the lookout, with things as they are in the world just now."

"You really think war will be declared before too much longer, don't you, Professor?" Mikael asked.

Bohr didn't answer directly.

"You're both coming to my birthday party next week, aren't you?" he asked. "Sophie, you have not yet seen inside the Mansion of Honor, my distinguished residence—it is quite over-the-top, really excessive for one man and his family to live in, but it is a wonderful place for a party! I think you will like it very much."

Back at the institute, as they walked upstairs—it was very late by now!—Sophie's thoughts wandered off in another direction. Why did she feel so ashamed of having seen Lilly abase herself to the mentalist? Was this notion of women wanting men to marry them, but only if they wanted to, a commonly held one? It struck Sophie, uneasily but forcefully, that she could imagine the state of mind that might prompt one to utter such a remark, but that she would rather undergo the most relentless inner and outer mortification than ever actually say such a thing. It was undoubtedly easier to talk about conspiracies and plots and politics than about what Sophie had come to call, sarcastically and only in her thoughts, *the mysteries of the human heart.*

Once they were ensconced in the sitting room with the mugs of hot cocoa that Fru Petersen inevitably pressed upon one to counteract the effects of the night air, and with the real, original Trismegistus settled along the back of the couch next to Sophie's head, Mikael said, "Sophie?"

"Yes?" she asked, flushing. She was glad he could not read her thoughts—she had been remembering the look on Lilly's face as her body strained toward the mentalist's.

"Since you've been here in København," he said uncertainly, "have you . . . you know . . . ?"

"No, what?"

"Have you been hearing the voices of the dead?"

"Oh, no," Sophie said, surprised. "At least, not so far as I've noticed—and I've been near all sorts of radios and telephones and so forth. There's been nothing at all anomalous, thank goodness. . . ."

"Why do you think that is, though, Sophie?" Mikael asked. "Do you think what happened in Edinburgh was—oh, I don't know what to call it—a one-off? Or is this, now, just a sort of interlude, a lull, and the whole thing might start up again at any time?"

"I hope it's more than a lull," Sophie said fervently. "I would be very glad never to have any such thing happen to me again! Thinking of what we saw in the darkroom that night sends shivers down my spine. And every time I make my mind blank so as to visualize the answer to a problem in geometry or algebra, I'm afraid I might be opening myself up to images transmitted from the mind of a dead person."

"Yes," Mikael said meditatively. "Sophie, don't misunderstand me; it's not that I question the reality of what we saw that night—rationally, I believe it really happened—but somehow, though it's not honestly all that long ago, I feel almost as if it must have been a dream. . . ."

"I know what you're saying," Sophie said. She let her fingers rest on Tris's lush coat. She liked the feel of the bones of the cat's shoulders, and the way they structured the whole shape of him in this particular configuration. "Mikael, do you really think that the mind-reading trick this evening was a simple matter of ventriloquism?"

"If it weren't so late at night," he said, "we could telephone the ventriloquists in the phone directory and see what they have to say for themselves!"

The actual day of Niels Bohr's birthday—October 7—had been declared a national holiday by the government, with Bohr's slightly mournful face and heavy brows also set to adorn a new postage stamp. (It had been a deliberate policy in the Hanseatic countries to legislate against the old preference for not representing a living person on currency or postage.) There was no news regarding Elsa Blix, and Sophie felt as though her hands were completely tied when it came to the investigation of the questions raised by Tabitha's letter. Her generally irritable mood that week was exacerbated on Tuesday afternoon by Fru Petersen making her try on a dark blue velvet party dress with a white lace collar. The daughter of one of Fru Petersen's friends had grown out of it; it fit Sophie perfectly.

"That's what you'll wear on Friday, then," Mikael's mother said with satisfaction. "Those ballet slippers will be fine, as far as shoes go, and I think you've still got a few pairs of tights without holes, haven't you, Sophie?"

"Yes, I suppose so," Sophie grumbled.

Sophie thoroughly rejected the notion that clothing should have a strongly decorative component—of course, some people liked to wear attention-getting things, but really it would be better if everyone just wore navy-blue boilersuits and stout leather boots and didn't have to worry about the silly convention of wearing different clothes on different days of the week and at different times of day or in different settings. Sophie had never been an unequivocal admirer of school uniforms, which she felt drew too much attention to natural differences between girls' looks—not just their figures but their general sense of style—but at least they let one blend in. Hanna Adler's school, because it was so "advanced," did not require uniforms, which meant that Sophie could wear a very similar dark-colored shirt and skirt and cardigan every day, and since all the clothes had been purchased in København by the stylish and sensible Fru Petersen, they enabled Sophie to achieve what seemed to her almost the only really worthwhile goal of clothing, namely not to stand out in a crowd.

She felt somewhat deceptive wearing the slippers, having never performed a step of ballet in her life, but they were much cheaper than other kinds of party shoe, and Fru Petersen had already persuaded her that it did not amount to a fraudulent misrepresentation to wear a piece of clothing strongly associated with an activity one did not practice, adducing as the clincher to her argument the facts that plus-four trousers were worn even by people who didn't play golf, and that Fru Petersen herself—Sophie was not really sure it was the same thing, but had allowed herself to be persuaded—had been known to use scientific glassware for making jam.

"If you really hate the dress, we can buy something new! Only it seems a pity to buy something you'll almost certainly grow out of without having worn more than a few times," Fru Petersen mused. "I'd rather see you spend the money on a really good-quality winter coat, with room to grow into it—we must go to the shops one of these upcoming weekends and see what they've got. Sophie?"

"The dress is perfectly fine," Sophie said hastily. "Really, you can choose anything you like for me; I am sure it will be nice enough, only I strongly prefer not to have to go shopping myself!"

"You sound just like Mikael!" Fru Petersen said.

"Will it be a nice party or a dull one?" Sophie asked.

"Dull," Fru Petersen said firmly, though her eyes were twinkling, "but I can promise you that there will be wonderful sweets!"

It was very cold all week, almost uncannily so, with record low temperatures for Denmark at that time of year. Trismegistus actually crept beneath the duvet that night and slept right up next to Sophie, after making it known, with an imperious dig of the claws, that he wished to situate himself *under* rather than *on*: a prepositional development more hospitable to warmth than to relaxation, as the cat stirred restively every time Sophie turned over to try to find a position comfortable enough to let her drift off.

Flurries of snow could be seen on Wednesday morning, and on Thursday after school so much snow fell that Mikael and Sophie borrowed a pair of tea trays from the lunchroom under the eaves and went and sledded on a modest hill nearby. It was surprising how much speed one could build up even on quite a short hill, and this particular one had a helpful flat section of packed snow at the bottom that allowed one to shoot off horizontally like a cork out of a well-aimed champagne bottle.

They were cold, wet, and a bit battered when they got back to the institute: Sophie would have a huge bruise on her hip the next day, and had tweaked some minor muscle in her side that made laughing slightly painful, but their exertions gave relish to the ample meal provided by Fru Petersen.

After they had both finished their homework, Sophie and Mikael found themselves leaning on the deep windowsill in the sitting room and watching the snow continue to fall outside in the cones of illumination the street lighting cast. København's first street lamps had been a seventeenth-century innovation spearheaded by the astronomer Ole

Rømer, who wanted to make the city safer by lighting its streets at the public's expense. Rømer had also made a set of observations that led to his being the first person to propose that light has a finite speed, a phenomenon for which he had coined a phrase almost more magical than anything Sophie had ever heard: *the hesitation of light.*

"The hesitation of light!" she said now, enjoying the feel of the words in her mouth and their sound in her ears.

"What?"

"Oh, nothing," she said, a little ashamed of the childish pleasure she took in the ring of certain words and phrases regardless of their meaning.

Arne had gone infuriatingly and elusively silent again. When would Sophie be invited to visit Nobel? She knew that Fru Petersen had several times tried to put a telephone call through to her older son, but he never seemed to be at home or at work at the times one would expect.

In the positive ledger column, though, Sophie had received a most amazing letter from Nan in which Nan expressed her absolute shock and surprise at learning the truth about IRYLNS and then gave Sophie almost the best news she could possibly have heard: Priscilla and Jean would not enter IRYLNS after all! The program was being disbanded, and no more girls would suffer the kind of damage that Sophie had witnessed on the locked ward: a turn of events that made Tabitha's death—Sophie had tried to ignore the thought, but honesty compelled her to admit it—seem almost worthwhile.

And what they will do now to stay useful, I cannot tell you, Nan had concluded of their two other school friends, with a barely suppressed outrage that had made Sophie rather want to laugh. *Priscilla has two offers of marriage on the table, and Jean is scheming to get sent overseas to join the secretarial staff at the Scottish embassy in Saint Petersburg!*

"A penny for your thoughts," Mikael said, drawing Sophie's attention back to him. It was an expression she had always found odd—what were its origins, she wondered, and had a penny originally been a generous offer or was it as meager as it sounded?

"We are going to a party tomorrow!" she said instead, feeling a rush of sudden and inexplicable happiness.

"Yes," said Mikael, regarding her with slight perplexity. "Are you looking forward to it, then, Sophie?"

"I have one word only: *cake*!"

"It's true, and I am sure it will be very good cake, too," Mikael said, moving toward her as if he were going to embrace her, then stopping at the last moment before their bodies touched. "Sophie . . ."

His voice trailed off. They stood very near each other, close but not touching, still leaning on their elbows on the windowsill and looking out at the falling snow.

Trismegistus broke the spell by twining around Sophie's ankles, giving a particularly piercing meow that reminded her she had meant to give him a saucer of milk.

"Are you two up still?" Fru Petersen said, coming into the room and drawing the curtains. The room felt smaller and more claustrophobic with the windows covered.

"Bedtime, I think," she added. "Tomorrow will be a late night."

The snow continued to fall heavily as the car dropped them at the foot of the grand staircase in front of Bohr's mansion. The stairs had been shoveled, but they were already accumulating a new layer of snow that accentuated the flimsy nature of Sophie's ballet slippers. The great vaulted front hallway offered a spectacle in cream and rose and gold, with enormous vases of flowers everywhere one turned. A servant took their coats, and while Mikael's mother tendered her felicitations to Bohr, Sophie and Mikael gravitated to the dining room, where a waiter with a silver ladle poured them tiny cut-glass cups of citrus punch from a crystal bowl with slices of oranges and lemons floating alongside bergs of ice.

As the noise mounted, Sophie and Mikael happily gorged themselves. Surely the main point of a grown-up party, if one were not yet quite grown-up oneself, was being allowed to stay up past one's bedtime and eat delicious things? The sideboards were almost groaning with hams and roast turkeys and whole sides of smoked salmon and the most delicious thin slices of brown bread and mounds of fresh salted butter and platters of cheese—in short, everything that Sophie, who liked food to be plain rather than mixed together, found utterly delicious.

The sweets had been set up in the conservatory, a palatial greenhouse separated from the dining room by a massive wall of plate glass through which could be seen a near-tropical profusion of greenery and bright birds and flowers.

"Shall we go and look at the cake selection?" Sophie said to Mikael, already slightly sick to her stomach from having overeaten and yet with the yen for something divinely sugary dancing on her tongue.

"Oh, yes, let's," Mikael agreed.

They stopped along the way to look at the lorikeets, whose bright plumage matched the brilliant pinks and reds and yellows of the flowers dotting the conservatory's lush greenery.

"Lavish!" Sophie said fervently.

A bird in the enclosed aviary came right up to the wire screen and looked inquisitively into her face to see whether she might give it something nice to eat, chirping in a questioning fashion when Sophie shook her head.

The jewel-colored jungle, with its damp, earth-smelling air and tropical warmth, was made extraordinarily more striking by the fact that outdoors the snow continued to fall: indeed, it fell so heavily that even a few feet away from the glass could be seen only a thick blanket of dull whiteness.

"When I was little," Mikael mused, "whenever it snowed, my grandmother would look out of the window and say, 'Those are the white bees swarming.' And when I asked her if the white bees had a queen and a hive, as ordinary bees do, she drew me a picture of the Snow Queen in her palace. . . ."

"The Snow Queen!"

"Yes—and you know, Sophie, it will sound far-fetched, but I could almost swear I saw her once or twice myself, with my own eyes, in real life, during the coldest bits of winter—a beautiful girl, quite tall—"

Sophie flinched slightly. Her small stature remained a point of sensitivity, and she could not hear someone else described as tall without feeling it obliquely as criticism; in her heart of hearts, despite the evident liking he had often expressed for Sophie, she believed that Mikael would prefer a tall girlfriend who was strikingly good-looking and with a lovely figure.

"—and draped all in a sort of white gauzy stuff, with a halo of bright white light around her head. She had bare feet, though it was awfully snowy, and they were just as smooth and alabaster-white as her face and hands. It made me shiver to look at her. She seemed almost as though she must be made of ice. . . ."

Just then the headmistress of Sophie's new school hove into view, in intent conversation with the geography teacher, who was Niels Bohr's sister. As Mikael and Sophie didn't want to have to make polite grown-up conversation, they hastily made their way to the darkest corner of the room and took up residence behind a fifteen-foot-tall rubber plant.

"How's your stomach doing, Sophie?" Mikael asked. "Ready for more food?"

"Surely it couldn't hurt just to go and *look* at the sweets," she said longingly.

They slipped around dense clusters of partygoers until they were right by the dessert table. Slivers of talk continued to intrude into Sophie's consciousness—Otto Robert Frisch and Hilde Levi were having a lively argument about the notion of quantum entanglement; Hevesy was rhapsodizing in strongly accented Danish about the nursery rhymes of his Hungarian childhood; two men who might have been diplomats or spies chattered in a high-speed Russian of which Sophie could understand just enough to be almost certain they were discussing which laundry did the best job starching shirts for the least amount of money.

Her ears might have strayed, but her eyes were wholly

captivated by the glory of the sight before them. There were platters divided into sections with dried apricots and cherries and cashews and candied ginger, and one plate after another of perfect little round chocolate truffles, each in an individual fluted paper cup and with all sorts of different decorations on top. The plainest ones were simply rolled in cocoa, while others were decorated with little caps of white chocolate with a light dusting of cinnamon or star-shaped patterns of silver and gold dragées.

There were heaping platters of hothouse fruit: green and purple seedless grapes with the blush still on them, apricots and peaches and plums, strawberries with a scent strong and sweet enough to cut through the competing aromas of chocolate and almond and vanilla and cigars and cognac and women's perfume and the rich, almost rotting smell of tropical flowers and earth.

The centerpiece, though, was an enormous multitiered silver cake stand piled with the most beautiful little cakes and pastries imaginable. There were miniature éclairs piped full of pastry cream and covered with shiny chocolate icing and perfect decorative white squiggles down the middle. There were pink macaroons sandwiched together with a light green pistachio cream and white ones sprinkled with coconut. There were tiny fairy cakes iced in the most perfect pale blues and pinks and lavenders, like a gorgeous sunset.

There were Lilliputian fruit tarts, their delicate custard filling topped with a few raspberries or miniature orange segments or strawberries and glistening with sugar glaze. There were heart-shaped linzer tortes and almond crescents and hazelnut *tuiles* and black-and-white checkerboard *sablés* and exquisite rosettes of butter cookies decorated with glacé cherries.

After agonizing over what to have first, Sophie finally chose a tiny cake iced in robin's-egg blue and covered with green and yellow sugar confetti. She ate it in two bites, relishing the airy taste of the buttercream icing and the almost fantastically light sponge base.

While she was deciding what to try next, Mikael put his hand on her arm and turned her gently toward the entrance hall. Around them, others were moving into the central hallway, and Mikael whispered to Sophie that the hour had come for the birthday toasts and speeches.

"Take a few sweets and wrap 'em in a napkin, and we'll find a good place to watch from!" he said.

While Mikael filled a napkin with macaroons and truffles, Sophie chose an almond-pear tart and a perfectly cubical pink-iced petit four with a candied rose petal on top. Mikael led her toward a side staircase and up to a landing that gave them a bit of elevation.

Sophie could hardly understand a word of the first speech,

a paean of praise in Danish from the head of the Carlsberg Brewery, on whose grounds the mansion stood and whose funds supported both Bohr and the scientific institute he directed. When she had first arrived in Denmark, Sophie had experienced the disconcerting illusion that everyone in the streets of København was actually speaking English, only an English become mysteriously incomprehensible to her, as though some lesion had taken away not only the language but also her ability to perceive the extent of the cognitive loss. Even now it seemed more plausible to Sophie that she had lost the ability to comprehend spoken English than that the brewery chairman was actually speaking a different language, so thoroughly did the sound and rhythms of Danish mimic the familiar English cadences.

Mikael shifted restlessly beside Sophie.

"This fellow's going to go on forever," he muttered. "We should have stocked up much more extensively on cakes!"

"Yes," Sophie whispered, "but really it will look too awful now if we go back over there during the birthday toasts."

At last the brewery chairman stopped speaking, urging everyone to raise their glasses and drink to Bohr's health. Bohr raised his glass—the light sparkled in the champagne.

"Sophie," Mikael began, but before he could say another word, Sophie found herself flat on the floor, the wind knocked out of her. The air was filled with a strange, sinister hissing sound and a popping and pinging like nothing she had ever heard before in her life, and over the babble of frantic voices could be heard the sound of a woman screaming.

She risked a glance at Mikael, who put his hand up to his face and touched a rivulet of blood running down from his temple to his chin, then looked at his fingers. He went very pale, a sort of whitish green, and began to sway. A moment later, he fell to the ground in a dead faint. She took his hand and began to say his name, not loudly but over and over again until someone came to help her away.

Part 2

October 1938

København and Elsinore, Denmark

Helsingborg and Stockholm, Sweden

The device had been propelled through the conservatory windows by a mobile rocket launcher found abandoned outside; though the police had swarmed the grounds, they had otherwise discovered only a trail of footprints—rapidly snowed over—leading to a lay-by off the main road. The perpetrator of the attack had made a getaway by car, and though the newspapers said that various leads were being pursued, Sophie suspected the police knew very little.

Mikael's flesh wounds were only superficial, but he and others from the institute who had breathed in large amounts of gas remained mostly unconscious since the attack. Several hundred guests had been affected in total, including many of Denmark's most prominent citizens; impromptu infirmaries had been set up all over the city—the institute's lunchroom had been given over to cots, with two full-time nurses—and a quarantine was imposed on everyone who had been at the party until a team of researchers from the school of public health could work out what had happened.

Quarantine! The word alone made Sophie think of bubonic plague and smallpox and the other grotesque afflictions pictured in the color plates of the encyclopedia of diseases of the skin that had revolted and mesmerized her as a child roaming the stacks of the University of Edinburgh library.

The gas seemed to have had a noticeable soporific and tranquilizing effect on many who breathed it in. Mikael had been much calmer immediately following the attack than Sophie (indeed, he was barely conscious), even as the nurse in the emergency tent—erected in a matter of minutes by a team of army medics, and heated with portable kerosene stoves—had used tweezers to remove the little pellets from his shoulder. She had placed each one carefully in a small metal kidney-shaped dish in which they rolled around like ball bearings; most of the metal was fairly near the surface, but several very deep pieces were left where they were, as it would do more damage poking around trying to remove them than leaving the flesh to heal.

As Mikael and the other victims slept, Sophie became increasingly convinced that her friend might never wake up again. What if Mikael had something like the sleeping sickness spread by the tsetse fly in Africa? What if he slept the whole rest of his life away? She pored over the newspaper each morning—a special section of the front page was now dedicated to the "Bohr Terror Report"—but found nothing conclusive.

There was only so much time she could spend doing the assignments that Miss Adler had sent over from school, and when Fru Petersen saw how frantic Sophie was getting, she sent her downstairs to Bohr's office to help with the typing again. Now even the corner shop had to be telephoned and asked to replenish the chocolate supply by leaving boxes on the doorstep—Sophie had not realized how much she took for granted the privilege of wandering out on a minor errand, and the institute felt almost as oppressive as a sarcophagus.

By Tuesday, the patients seemed significantly more wakeful, and when Mikael sat up in bed and said he was hungry, Sophie—who had been sitting and rereading *David Copperfield* by his bedside—was so moved and relieved that she could hardly speak. She ran to find Fru Petersen, who had, of course, been cooking all sorts of delicious convalescent foods that she and Sophie could barely swallow. Sophie had never felt as strong a fellow feeling with Fru Petersen as when they sat across the dining table and gazed at Mikael eating two huge plates of stewed beef and half a loaf of rye bread with thick slatherings of butter. It was the most beautiful sight Sophie had ever seen.

The day after, Mikael's convalescence continued to advance, and he and Sophie spent the morning playing various card games, and then checkers and backgammon. Sophie's initial relief at having Mikael back, though, had turned to something more troubling.

Mikael was not himself.

Oh, he could think and talk clearly enough; it was not that his cognitive faculties had been impaired. His physical energy had largely returned, too—if anything, he seemed more energetic and restless than usual, tiring after a while of sedentary games and instead kicking a ball around the attic room until it bumped up against the sideboard so hard that a china plate was knocked off and smashed on the floor.

The plate had been a particular favorite of Sophie's. It featured five strangely geometrical roosters strategically interspersed with haystacks and farming implements against a Chinese-style background and with a very beautiful border of different shades of green, everything from tangy bright apple to lush emerald and the bright, sharp color of early spring grass.

Sophie was aghast, but Mikael only laughed.

A medical assessment in the Bohr Terror Report had noted that one striking symptom among those recovering from the effects of the gas attack—the precise chemical constituents still had not been identified—was an emotional affect of recklessness and indifference to the feelings of others. The thought of chemistry affecting personality disturbed Sophie, and she found it worrying to think of Mikael as part of an afflicted cohort, all somehow transformed—at least for a little while—into impulsive creatures immune from the normal promptings of regret or remorse. The doctors had no clue why some people should have been so strongly influenced by the chemicals while others remained impervious, but the phenomenon was widespread, with men roughly four times more likely than women to have had their behavior transformed.

Fru Petersen was downstairs, in the thick of the logistical nightmare of trying to keep the essential scientific functions of the institute going under quarantine conditions while also supplying everyone with food and amusement. When she came back upstairs and saw the broken plate, she said nothing, only gathered up the pieces and said calmly that she would take it downstairs and see whether someone in one of the workshops might rivet it back together.

"I don't know why you'd bother with that," Mikael said dismissively.

Sophie's eyes filled with tears, though his contempt had

not been directed specifically at her.

Fru Petersen did not look hurt. Her lips pursed in a way that Sophie suddenly realized meant that she was so angry she could hardly speak.

The only thing she did, though, was to say after a moment that there was a very good cake downstairs in the reception area of Bohr's office—his secretary had ordered it from a bakery to try to cheer him up—and they could each have a piece if they got there while there was some left. Bohr, too, was quarantined, of course, but he had been allowed a special vehicle for moving back and forth between the Mansion of Honor and the institute. It was marked with a rather frightening hazard sign on both doors, the traditional poison symbol of skull and crossbones in black and a bright, bilious yellow so lurid one felt it might even glow in the dark.

Sophie and Mikael went back downstairs with Fru Petersen for cake. Bohr was closeted in his office for an important telephone call, and the atmosphere outside seemed tense, but it was certainly a very nice-looking cake, a rectangular one with two chocolate layers bursting with whipped cream and cherry jam and an utterly lavish top bit that had lots of very rich chocolate icing of a kind that Sophie believed might be called ganache and a gorgeous pattern of white piped latticework and little pink and red roses tucked in around the edges. Sophie rather had her eye on a particularly good pink one.

When Mikael danced ahead of Sophie and cut himself a huge piece of cake, she thought nothing of it, but what he did next astounded her. She would not, of course, have minded had he taken the next bit of rose for himself. Sophie always felt slightly ashamed of her greediness with respect to cake: really, any piece of cake should be just as good as another, though it was strongly written into her nature to covet a corner piece with an icing flower.

But rather than either taking the rose with his own slice or leaving it for Sophie, Mikael first cut carefully around it, then took a fork from the supply of cutlery the secretary had placed beside the cake and, giving Sophie an impudent look, used the fork to smash the icing rose and grind it down into the cardboard bakery tray.

He laughed at the expression on Sophie's face, and then forked off the last cluster of roses remaining on top of the cake and popped it into his mouth, smacking his lips with ostentatious pleasure.

"Mikael!" Sophie said, stricken, but he went on laughing heartlessly at her evident distress.

She tried to control her emotions as she cut her own piece of cake, but she felt quite dazed as she climbed the stairs after Mikael. She found that she could not force down more than a few bites, and put the plate and fork back on the table.

Mikael had already finished his own slice, but he now helped himself to Sophie's without asking, finishing the rest of it in a few mouthfuls.

She did not realize, until the tears were actually rolling down her cheeks, how very upset she was. She sniffed unattractively and tried to stop, but instead found herself crying harder.

"Why are you crying, Sophie?" Mikael asked. "It makes you look quite awful. Your eyes are all red!"

"What's happened to you, Mikael?" Sophie sobbed, trying to snuffle up some of the awful crying-related snot that was about to pour out of her nose. Oh, if only she were the kind of person who really reliably carried a handkerchief!

"There's nothing the matter with me," said Mikael. "It's bunk, what they're saying in the papers about the attack—if anything, I feel better than I ever have before in my life. Stop crying, you idiot!"

They were interrupted a second time by Fru Petersen.

"You had better turn on the radio," she said to Mikael.

Sophie was afraid that he would refuse to do so, but after a moment he got up and turned on the apparatus in the corner of the sitting room, then went over to the casement window and began swinging it in and out on its hinge, the cold air coming into the room and blowing away a sheaf of papers that had been stacked in a neat pile on the desk.

Trismegistus had stalked into the room behind Fru Petersen, and Sophie, though she always felt it to be a slight affront to his dignity, picked him up and settled him down on her knee, pressing her hands into his thick fur for comfort. She could feel the steady vibration of his purr, a deep, reassuring rumble that seemed to resonate with her own sympathetic nervous system and helped her settle down into some semblance of calm.

The radio was tuned to the English-language news station. The journalist Sophie liked best, an English refugee named Eric Blair, whose thoughts on politics and language seemed more interesting to Sophie than almost anything she had ever heard, was reporting from a spot near København harbor.

The noise in the background was unbelievable—aeroplanes buzzing around overhead, the sounds of sirens and of blaring radios and people milling in the streets. It provided a strangely disorienting accompaniment to Blair's calm reporting. He painted a picture of unmarked European troop ships moving in during the early morning darkness and under cover of fog and passing by the harbor forts, the security forces there having been paid off not to alert the Danish army to what was going on: paid off or, more likely, Blair said grimly, manipulated by way of their sympathies for the notion of a European-backed government committed to the strong enforcement of a rule of law.

Small groups of elite forces had then dispersed with great rapidity throughout the city—to the army headquarters, to the palace where parliament was in session—a parliament that had scrambled to come up with a plan and that, before an hour had passed, had voted in favor of a policy of nonresistance.

Now it was lunchtime, and the European occupation of Denmark was official.

Aeroplanes marked with the distinctive Napoleonic insignia could be heard flying overhead, Blair continued, and were dropping leaflets intended to indoctrinate those who read them. These manifestos stated that the federation's troops did not set foot on Danish soil as enemies; that European military operations were aimed exclusively at protecting a vulnerable Denmark from the onslaught of a possible Russian invasion; that Europe had no intention of infringing on the territorial integrity and political independence of her Danish neighbor, or indeed on the independence of any other Hanseatic state; in short, that the people of Denmark would be wise not to offer any resistance.

"So the attack at the party really does seem to have been the precursor to a full-scale invasion," Sophie said, more to herself than to the others.

"It seems that way," Fru Petersen agreed.

"Will Blair be able to keep broadcasting if the Europeans really have occupied Denmark?" Sophie asked her.

"I doubt it," said Fru Petersen. "This may well be the last we hear of him, at least from Danish soil. If he can get out of the country in time, he may be able to resume broadcasting from Sweden or Finland."

"And—"

Sophie was about to ask another question, but Fru Petersen put her finger to her lips.

"Sophie, listen," she said urgently. "You, too, Mikael: this is of the utmost importance. I've been in consultation all this week with Niels Bohr, and we are in agreement as to what must happen next. We still haven't heard from Arne vis-à-vis Nobel's plans for Sophie, but we feel that there may be only a very small window of time in which Sophie, as a foreign national, will safely be able to get out of the country. It might be alarmist, but her visa situation is unusual, and there has been talk of the Europeans—it certainly has happened in Poland and Lithuania—putting foreigners and other undesirables into internment camps. The quarantine has been lifted, though we expect a curfew to be imposed shortly. Lise Meitner and her nephew are traveling to Stockholm tonight—Bohr and I believe that the two of you must go with them."

"On our bicycles, I suppose," Mikael said sarcastically.

"Indeed, on your bicycles, at least for part of the way," his mother agreed, ignoring the tone of his voice. "They will be put onto a rack on the roof of the car that will take you to Elsinore for the ferry. Meitner and Frisch will be met off the boat by a relative of theirs who will drive them to Stockholm, but the other seats in that car have already been promised to several old ladies who are not able to travel on their own, so you will have to cover the final leg of the trip by bicycle."

"But where will we go?" Sophie asked. She hoped Trismegistus would be amenable to being packed into the basket on her bike—it was certainly out of the question to leave him behind.

"To Arne, in Stockholm, of course," Fru Petersen said briskly. "He has a perfectly good set of rooms, and he has already obtained his landlady's permission to have you there as long as is needed."

"I know it is a difficult question for you to answer, but how long might that be?" Sophie asked anxiously.

Fru Petersen shook her head.

"It's impossible to say, Sophie," she said.

It did not take long to pack. Fru Petersen said to leave behind almost everything except for the bare urgent necessities, and that she would arrange for Sophie's and Mikael's clothes and books to be shipped directly to Arne's, assuming such shipping was still legal under the new regime. She sewed banknotes into the hem of Sophie's coat and the inner lining of Mikael's jacket, and finally told them to go and leave her alone to finish sorting everything out, as they were giving her fits by being so much underfoot while she tried to work!

They would leave at eight that evening. Under ordinary conditions, one might reach Elsinore in less than an hour by car, but it would certainly take much longer than that tonight. The ferry left every hour, though, and ran all through the night, so they would take whatever one they could.

In the meantime, Sophie and Mikael clattered downstairs to see what was going on. The library was off-limits—it was serving as a dormitory for patients no longer ill enough to need the infirmary but not well enough to return to their own lodgings. Bohr was much too busy to be interrupted, and the ground-floor auditorium had been given over to a fierce and argumentative blackboard-style debate among chalk-wielding physicists—Frisch and Meitner were both there, but too immersed in the cloud of symbols on the board to notice Sophie and Mikael at the door.

In the basement they found Hevesy and Hilde Levi at work. On the face of it, things here were so exactly as they always were that Sophie was able to forget for a moment how upside down everything had been turned by the invasion. Miss Levi was tabulating a set of data, and Hevesy himself was engaged in some sort of chemical procedure.

Then Sophie saw that before Hevesy on the countertop was an actual heap of gold medals.

"The Nobel Prize medals!" Mikael cried out.

He moved to them, almost involuntarily, and picked them up, cupping them in his hands and then turning his gaze on the Hungarian scientist.

"What are you doing with them?" he asked accusingly.

"Bohr has been worrying about what will happen if an occupying army finds them here," Hevesy said, carefully measuring out five hundred milliliters of acid and pouring the beaker of liquid into a jar with a seal. "These medals belong to various members of the institute, all of them Europeans who directly contravened the federation law that prohibits gold from being taken out of the empire. Their names are engraved into their respective medals, of course, and Bohr is worried that the discovery of the medals might have very serious consequences for the individuals concerned."

"Are you going to hide them?" Mikael asked.

"At first I suggested that we should bury them in the back garden," Hevesy confessed, "but Bohr was concerned that they might be too easily unearthed. So instead I am dissolving them in acid—I will hide them, as it were, in plain view."

As they watched, he detached the first medal from its

ceremonial ribbon and plopped it into the acid, where it began rapidly to dissolve.

"I will put the bottle on a shelf," he added, "and even the most suspicious intruder will have no idea what it is."

Miss Levi had paused in her work to give Hevesy a long glance of affection and amusement.

"You needn't sound so gleeful," she said, "even if it is a chemist's dream come true! Sophie, are you going to go to Sweden with the others?"

"Yes, Mikael and I both are," Sophie said regretfully. She felt the tears spring into her eyes and shook her head to make them go away. At almost any other time in the past few years, a trip with Mikael would have been absolute heaven, but now she feared she would be traveling with a virtual stranger.

"Safe travels, then," Miss Levi said, standing and coming to give Sophie a parting embrace. "Mikael, you will look out for Sophie, won't you?"

Mikael was poking at the macaw with a stick and didn't respond, but Sophie hugged Miss Levi tightly and promised that she and Mikael would look out for each other.

"When the war is over," said Hevesy thoughtfully, "we will mint the medals again."

"But they won't be the same medals!" Sophie cried out.

"It depends upon how you define the word *same*," said Hevesy. "If I call a place 'home,' does that simply mean the place where I live? What if I call more than one place home—and what if the first and foremost place I think of when I hear the word *home* no longer exists in the world, but only in my memory?"

They stood and looked at the jar of acid. The medals had vanished. One would never have known the gold continued to exist in any way, shape, or form.

The name Elsinore was romantic to Sophie because of Hamlet, the character and the play, but whatever turrety erections might grace the Danish coastline, the trip that night was so chaotic, and the evening so dark and overcast, that Sophie was left with only the vaguest impression of crenellations and looming battlements. The drive had taken longer than one would have thought possible, giving credence to Mikael's gripe—repeated so many times that Otto Robert Frisch finally told him to hold his tongue—that they would have been faster on their bicycles, which were strapped to the car's roof. In the backseat, Sophie clutched the basket holding Trismegistus to her chest.

The roads were packed, not just with cars but with carriages and horse-drawn carts and bicycles attached to homemade trailers and people walking on foot and pushing things in perambulators or shopping carts, all determined to escape the country before the anticipated crackdown on border crossing. When they arrived at Elsinore, they learned that the ferries for hours to come were already sold out. They finally got places on the five-o'clock boat, and spent the brief early-morning journey drinking very nasty hot chocolate topped by an unappealing form of whipped cream that Mikael said—Sophie had never heard the term before—was *ersatz*. Mikael seemed withdrawn and quiet, but Sophie found this less worrying than the bursts of manic energy that had characterized his behavior in the time since his recovery.

The doctors still hadn't worked out the exact nature of the chemicals in the attack, or whether the vicious little metal pellets had been intended to do anything more than collateral damage, but changes similar to the ones Sophie could see in Mikael continued to be observed in many others who had been present at the party. Nobody knew whether the effects would wear off in time or whether they would be permanent, and Sophie had already come to think of Mikael as containing something like Jekyll and Hyde's two selves—a stomach-churning prospect.

When they disembarked onto Swedish soil at Helsingborg, the lines for getting papers checked were very long, and Sophie was dismayed to find, once they had finally cleared customs and immigration, that they were due to part ways with their traveling companions immediately.

She had not really slept the night before, other than a

frigid, stiff hour or so in the car en route to Elsinore, and she was not at all sure that she had the mental fortitude for the long bicycle ride—it was about thirty miles to Stockholm—but Mikael told her to buck up, and Trismegistus supplemented the brusque instruction with a plangent, imperative meow that made Sophie laugh and think that perhaps she could do it after all. The cat was as heavy again as Sophie's modest luggage, but once everything was properly balanced, Sophie felt fully capable of managing it, especially as Tris seemed to understand that it made things easier when he did *not* yowl as they went round a corner.

Mikael consulted his pocket atlas regularly. They stopped, too, for him to repair a puncture in his front tire. While she waited, Sophie drank some of the glass thermal bulb of tea that Fru Petersen had instructed them to refill on the boat. Once Mikael had finished patching his tube—and drunk his own share of tea and eaten the other half of the rather sickly bar of Swiss chocolate Sophie had bought at the refectory in the ferry terminal—they got back on their bikes and continued along their way.

It was nearly dark by the time they arrived at Mr. Petersen's lodgings. The building was in a bleak outskirt of Stockholm, with grand but slightly dingy buildings and boulevards with the air of having rather come down in the world. Arne had left word with his landlady to let them in but was not himself home from work yet, which hit Sophie with a pang. It was unpleasant to think of feeling almost afraid at the prospect of being alone with Mikael.

Mikael would share his brother's bedroom, sleeping on a cot in the corner, and Sophie was relieved to learn that rather than being relegated to the sitting room couch, as she had at first feared, Mr. Petersen had arranged for the landlady to give Sophie a bedroom of her own in another part of the house.

It was a dank little room, with a strong smell of tobacco and a mysteriously greasy sheen on everything, and one had to go out into the hallway to use the toilet, but there was a sink in the corner, in which Sophie now very thankfully brushed her teeth. She fell into bed with all her clothes still on.

Sometime later she heard indistinct murmurs outside the bedroom door, but whoever it was must have decided it would be better to let Sophie sleep. Though she woke several times during the night in an utter panic, with no idea where she was and a strong sense of imminent danger, she was able to go back to sleep each time. Finally the combination of full daylight outside, a sharp feeling of hunger, and the pressure on her bladder prompted her to throw back the covers and brave the world outside these four walls.

She had somehow forgotten where to find the toilet and had to try several different doors, with a sick, nervous feeling of shyness, only overwhelming need forcing her to persist. Once she found the lavatory and had splashed water on her face and brushed her teeth, though, she felt considerably better. She left her sponge bag in her bedroom and went in search of Mikael and sustenance.

She found Mikael surrounded by the detritus of breakfast and a huge heap of partially disassembled newspapers. He looked up briefly and greeted her, and told her to ring the bell for Arne's landlady, who appeared immediately and promised to bring Sophie eggs, toast, and tea.

In the meantime Sophie began to leaf through the bits of the paper that Mikael had finished with, but was disappointed to find that many of them were in Swedish, and that her basic Danish could do little for her.

Mikael tossed over some pages of the English- and French-language coverage he was currently perusing, from which Sophie was able to glean that Denmark was now officially occupied. Perhaps as many as a hundred thousand people had left the country before the borders were closed that morning; the general of the European forces had promised that while a small number of people would be interned, every effort would be made to accommodate the Danish people and their national traditions and preferences.

"Arne was here for a bit this morning," Mikael said.

Sophie had finished eating her breakfast and was drinking a second cup of tea.

"You should have woken me!" Sophie said.

"He thought you needed the sleep," said Mikael. "He'll be back later this evening, in any case, though he told us not to wait for him to have supper."

Sophie looked round at the shabby furnishings and the gray skies outside.

"Do we have to stay here, or can we go out?" she asked.

"Once the landlady gives us a key, we can do what we like," Mikael said. "It's a lark! Oh, I'm sure that by next week we'll have been sorted out with some kind of school—Arne's going to visit the headmaster of the English school and see if they have room for us both in the sixth form."

"Won't we go and see Alfred Nobel first, though?" Sophie asked, feeling unsettled by her lack of familiarity with the setting and the routine here. "He must live quite nearby, mustn't he?"

Mikael didn't know.

"I've been out already," he added, "to explore the neighborhood. It's a bit quiet, but I'm sure we'll find things to do—we're not that far from the center of town, really. Let's go!"

"I must have a bath first," Sophie said fervently. Breakfast was a very good thing—she felt considerably more human than she had upon first getting up—but the sheer greasy griminess of her skin was making it impossible to greet her current predicament with equanimity.

"Oh, what a bother, Sophie," Mikael grumbled. "Must

you really? The morning's half-gone already!"

But he rang the bell, and the landlady came in and whisked Sophie off with her. Strange to say, she was a very pleasant Scottish lady called Mrs. McGregor. She had some sort of family connection with the Petersens and had been letting rooms in Stockholm for at least three decades, but was still very proud of the Scottish connection, telling Sophie that she was a native of Edinburgh and how good it was to hear another Scottish voice.

The bathroom was cold and cavernous, and the towels rather threadbare, but the hot water was very hot indeed and came forth in ample quantities. Having put on a clean set of underpants and a vest, Sophie did not find it overly penitential to put back on the trousers and wool jumper she had been wearing before. The clean socks in particular were bliss—socks became somehow almost *crusty* if one wore them for more than one day. It was unsavory to contemplate.

It was beginning to get dark by the time Sophie was dressed again, and she resisted Mikael's entreaties for her to come outside with him. He went without her, and she was left to regret her choice—there was very little of interest to read, and she had too much time to sit and fret about what might be happening back at the institute.

What if Europe decided to ignore Sweden's neutrality and invade the country anyway, en route to complete domination of all the formerly independent Hanseatic states? Scotland must be in danger, too—the papers had reported nothing in particular about a European initiative in that direction, but it did not seem at all plausible that the armies of the federation would not soon have a stab at it, though Sophie felt sure that her compatriots, unlike the Danish, would go down fighting rather than allow for a bloodless occupation.

And what if Mikael—but the thought did not bear contemplating!—never returned to his true self?

Mrs. McGregor gave them supper—cock-a-leekie soup, ham sandwiches, and a delicious apple pie—and they sat for a time afterward in Mr. Petersen's sitting room. It was after nine o'clock by the time Arne got home, and he seemed very tired and not at all inclined to provide nonlaconic answers to the barrage of questions that Sophie and Mikael leveled at him.

"Does your mother know we've arrived safely?"

"Yes."

"Can I borrow your ice skates?"

"No."

"Why not?"

"Wrong size."

"Snowshoes, then?"

"Yes."

"Has a time been set, now that I'm here, for me to go

and speak with Alfred Nobel?"

"No."

"If I am snowshoeing, where is the best place for me to get a run at a nice clean stretch of snow?"

Finally Mrs. McGregor made them leave Arne alone while he ate his supper.

Sophie couldn't get to sleep that night. She had slept too long the night before, she supposed, and she felt fretful and out of sorts, so physically and mentally tired—with sore bicycling muscles to boot!—that at moments, as she tossed and turned and tried to find a comfortable position, she wondered if she would ever be able to fall asleep again. It was not so much how awful one felt the day after a sleepless night that was the problem as the sheer horror of having to greet a new day without a decent period of unconsciousness to separate it from the previous one.

Tris didn't help. Sophie had set up a tray of litter for him in the corner of her bedroom for when he couldn't go outside, and bowls of food and water under the washbasin, but his sporadic investigative padding around was broken up by intervals in which he kneaded her stomach with his paws and batted at her feet. The chiming of the hours by the grandfather clock in the hallway downstairs only deepened Sophie's despair.

She finally fell into a restless doze sometime after four,

which meant she woke late again, well after nine o'clock. By the time she had bathed and dressed and breakfasted and given her underclothes to Mrs. McGregor for the laundry, Mikael was pacing back and forth like a caged panther; he had dug out all of his brother's winter gear and found it in such a condition of disuse and disrepair that most of it was actually now literally unusable, including the snowshoes.

"Let us go sledding," he said finally, having thrown aside a heap of gear in disgust.

Sophie could not feel any fire in her belly at the prospect of sledding, but she went obediently with Mikael to beg a pair of metal trays from Mrs. McGregor, who found them a couple whose advanced state of battering meant they could come to no further harm. They bundled up with scarves and gloves and boots and went outside to find a good hill.

The day was gray and overcast, with the feeling of snow in the air, but even the damp grayness was refreshing after the slightly claustrophobic warmth of Mr. Petersen's sitting room. The park nearby had a very decent bank on which some younger children were already sledding, and Mikael and Sophie had a few runs down it, which Sophie genuinely enjoyed, especially the bit where they shot off the bottom and came gradually to a standstill, spinning to a stop only at the very edge of the park.

Some older boys soon joined the pack of sledders, though,

and Sophie watched regretfully as they tired of sledding and instead initiated a complex and virtually paramilitary game of snowballing whose unarticulated rules seemed byzantine and whose physical requirements were well beyond Sophie's capacities. After a little while, finding herself on the periphery and with the feeling of being about to burst into tears at any moment—the last snowball had hit her directly in the face, a hard-packed icy projectile flung by a tall boy who had laughed at her expression and then run off to pelt someone else—she looked around for Mikael. She did not want to spoil his pleasure—he could be happy here for hours more—but she felt in need of home.

"Don't let's leave, Sophie," Mikael said, adding thoughtfully, "I know you're not much of a thrower, but you could perfectly well make me a good magazine of snowballs. I am finding it difficult to keep my arsenal stocked."

Sophie regretfully declined.

"Well, I'm staying," he said, "even if you're not."

It was a frigid and gloomy walk back to the lodging house. At one point, she became afraid that she had lost her way, and though she felt an awful baby, she could not stop a few tears from rolling over the bottoms of her eyelids. The taste of salt comforted her, though, and it was an amazing relief to realize that she was on the right street after all, indeed only a few houses from home.

She had her own key, and she let herself in and crept up

to her room, where she took off her wet things and hung them over the back of a chair and slid back into bed in her underthings, to be joined under the duvet by Trismegistus.

Mikael seemed inexhaustibly and impossibly boisterous when he finally got home. Oblivious to Sophie's anxieties (she had dragged herself out of bed and back into her clothes), he was instead full of news of a shop where they would mend the bindings on Arne's cross-country skis.

"And they have used boots, too, marked down to very reasonable prices, including a pair just my size," he concluded triumphantly.

"Do you think I would like cross-country skiing?" Sophie asked timidly.

"You? Sophie, don't make me laugh! You hate all that sort of thing—and besides, it will slow me down awfully if you come with me—much better if you give it a miss."

Even in light of how cruel he'd been since awakening from the artificial sleep following the attack at Bohr's party, Mikael's discouraging words were unexpected enough that Sophie's breath caught in her throat. Mikael had been such a stalwart supporter even of Sophie's slightly hopeless endeavors to become a competent cyclist. Had he hated every ride they'd ever taken together because of Sophie's slowness?

Tris had been sitting grooming himself in the corner, but as Mikael spoke to Sophie, the cat had pricked up his ears and then lifted himself up and trotted over to Mikael and sniffed him. Then the cat bristled and began hissing, back arched, the fur all over his body puffed up, his tail an enormous bottlebrush.

Mikael seemed unsettled by the cat's fury. He scooped the cat up in the damp towel he had been using to dry his hair and tossed him out into the corridor, then slammed the door after him. The cat was left to meow plaintively and fruitlessly in the hall for readmission.

Arne was late coming home again, and the conversation played out almost exactly as it had the night before, with Sophie—she was trying not to sound grumbly, but feared the attempt was not a success—asking whether there was any arrangement for her to see Nobel and Arne looking weary and slightly annoyed and telling Sophie that the latest developments in the war meant that Nobel had almost more on his plate than he could manage, and that Sophie must be patient.

"Look!" Mikael shouted.

Sophie and Arne were still finishing their puddings, but Mikael had not been able to stay at the table.

"I can walk on my hands!"

"Not inside, please!" said his brother, but Mikael had already thrown himself heels over head and begun to walk around the room on his hands.

Trismegistus yowled and shot out of the room like a

rocket. Mikael came to grief a moment later, overbalancing directly onto a little table with a china box on it. Everything crashed to the ground; one leg of the table splintered, and the box smashed into tiny pieces.

Mikael was not at all penitent. It was Arne who apologized to Mrs. McGregor and who spent the rest of the evening sitting at the dining table, newspaper laid out before him to protect the surface of the table, mixing little patches of adhesive and applying the fixative with a matchstick to the china, then devising a cunning sort of brace to hold the pieces together while they dried.

Just as he finished, the telephone in the hallway began to ring. A moment later, Mrs. McGregor came to find him.

"There's a call for you, Mr. Petersen," she said. "I think it's work—the gentleman sounds quite urgent."

Arne went to answer the call. Sophie couldn't hear what he was saying, just the low, infrequent murmur of his voice in response to the caller's longer stints of talking; she would have said the tone was resistance shading into resignation.

When he came back, he looked very sorry.

"Sophie, I must travel to the countryside tomorrow," he said, "to assess a situation that has transpired at one of Nobel's factories: a sabotage attempt has led to a great deal of trouble, and I must get there as soon as I can."

"Will we come with you?" Sophie asked, hoping very

much that this would be the case.

"No," Arne said gently, "you'll be better off here, where I know Mrs. McGregor will keep an eye on you and feed you and so forth. And you've got my brother. . . ."

"Yes," said Sophie, feeling disconsolate. Loyalty should prevent her from saying it, but she could not help herself from adding the words under her breath: "Only he has been so *awful* recently! He has not been the same since the birthday party. . . ."

Arne gave her an inquisitive look.

"The papers have not used the word," she said impulsively, "but it is hard not to think of some kind of brainwashing—clearly his thought processes have been affected by the chemicals he inhaled, or even by those little metal pellets. The way he's acting—it's not his true self!"

"It should be that he'll calm down a bit once he's been here for a few days," Arne said, though Sophie could tell he was very worried. "I'll see if I can find a suitable doctor to check him out. There's no doubt that the attack was meant to make the population receptive for the next stage of the invasion, and though I know mind control is often considered a matter of science fiction rather than science fact, I wouldn't rule out the possibility that those affected may be more vulnerable than before to certain kinds of suggestion, hypnotic or otherwise."

"How long will you be gone?" Sophie asked.

"Oh, a week or so—not longer than that, anyway."

"A full week?" Sophie asked, her voice small and hopeless. "Surely you'll be back before next weekend?"

"I don't think so," Arne said. "Look, Sophie, if anything really strange happens, or even if you're just worried, you can easily put a call through to my mother. She'll tell you what she thinks—she knows Mikael better than anyone else, and she's also there on the spot to see how the other victims are recovering. I'll leave you plenty of money. There's a cinema around the corner if you get bored—I know it's not always easy waiting endless hours for something to happen—and Mrs. McGregor will give you all your meals. I can be reached by telephone, too, at least with a message, though it may take me some hours to return your call—I'm likely to be all over the place rather than working out of an office or a hotel room with really reliable telephone contact."

Arne was gone before Sophie even woke up the next morning. She had meant to get up in time to say good-bye to him, and she ate her breakfast in glum and self-reproachful silence.

Mikael was planning a frenetic day of exploration. He had mapped out the route they would take down to the water and across the bridge to the old town.

Sophie was not really in the mood, but on the premise that she would almost certainly be sorry if she stayed behind, she put on her warmest clothes and boots and followed him out into the street.

It was a long, cold walk down to the harbor, but the beauty of the city along the water made the trip well worth it. There were some obvious similarities to København: Stockholm had the strongly northern feel that characterized all of the major Hanseatic cities, including Edinburgh, with their situation on the water and their stern, slightly otherworldly northern beauty. But Stockholm also had a magnificent imperial aura quite unlike the style of København or Edinburgh. One got a strong sense here of Sweden's past as the dominant force in the Baltic, the city's grandeur surpassing even København's parade of forts and palaces.

They stood for a while watching the traffic on the water. Sweden's vaunted neutrality in the conflict between Europe and the other members of the Hanseatic League did not mean that the country was not arming herself as a precaution, and the whole area teemed with uniformed personnel and troop ships.

After a little while, they found themselves getting quite cold, so they crossed the bridge into the old town. Gamla Stan was a lovely warren of lanes, brightly colored shops, and houses that must have looked almost the same six hundred years earlier in medieval times, during the original period of Hanseatic dominance. Mikael, who had a map, steered them in the direction of a shop, where he purchased a small sled that he assured Sophie would be significantly superior to the tea trays for downhill purposes.

There was no point getting it wrapped, of course, and Mikael didn't want to wait to have it delivered to their lodgings. The sled had a kind of tether, so he wrapped the cord around his wrist and they set off down the street with the sled trailing behind them.

Sophie thought it looked uncomfortable and inconvenient, but hated herself for the dispiriting tone of her reflections. Perhaps it wasn't so much Mikael who had changed as Sophie herself! What if it was she who had become more timid and fearful, rather than Mikael more boisterous and heedless of her feelings?

The delicious smell of street food was pricking her nostrils, and when Mikael bought them each a sausage in a bun and asked Sophie, after she had polished hers off, whether she would like another, she felt his generosity as a guilty confirmation of her worst fears about her own Princess-and-the-Pea-like oversensitivity.

They had come into a beautiful open square, the space almost magically blossoming out of the warren of narrow streets. It had begun to snow again, and the combination of the soft flakes in the air, which felt a bit warmer than earlier, and the gray cobblestones underfoot and the grand three- and four-story buildings with their elegant facades struck

Sophie as almost intolerably beautiful. She felt winded by the intensity of the emotion that surged through her in the face of this prospect.

"Sophie?" Mikael said in a curious voice—either excited or upset, she couldn't tell which.

"What?"

"Look at the sign across the way—that's the Nobel Museum!"

Indeed, as they approached the banner closely enough to read the smaller lettering, they found that the grand palatial building Sophie had just been contemplating was in fact the Stockholm base for Nobel Enterprises Ltd. Though much of the building housed offices that were not open to the public, and that were probably not in any case very interesting to look at, the ground floor held a collection of singular historic interest touching on the invention of dynamite, the techniques used to process it, and the purposes to which it was put worldwide. There were also exhibits honoring the various men and women who had been awarded the Nobel Foundation's prestigious annual prizes; disconcertingly, one of the pictures reproduced in the exterior advertising was a very good photograph of Niels Bohr gesticulating wildly with his hands at the front of the ground-floor auditorium at the institute.

It was nice and warm inside. They checked their coats

and scarves and gloves at the cloakroom, where the attendant was also so obliging as to take custody of Mikael's sled, and walked quickly through the rooms. There was not a great deal to see, but it was of considerable interest, especially the pictures of so many people they knew from the institute: Pauli, Dirac, Hevesy, Meitner. Sophie felt a surge of pride at this irrefutable evidence that intellectual eminence in physics was not exclusively the preserve of men, and spared a thought to hope that Lise Meitner and her nephew had arrived safely at their destination.

Afterward they bought cups of cocoa at the small tearoom in back of the museum, but Mikael was keen to get back outdoors. Sophie went to use the ladies' lavatory, then sought out her friend in the central hall. She found him near the exit and gazing at an almost ceremonial spectacle taking place some feet away. Perhaps as many as a dozen executives from the offices upstairs—one could tell they were important people by the way their suits were cut and from their curiously uniform, fair, pink, prosperous look—were gathered in a sort of pack around the figure of someone Sophie guessed must be a visiting dignitary.

"Look at her!" Mikael breathed. "Why, she's utterly magnificent!"

The object of his admiration was a tall woman—over six feet, and slender as a birch tree—dressed in a long white fur coat over a white trouser suit and white leather boots. From behind, she looked like an apparition from a modern fairy tale—indeed, she could easily have been the Snow Queen of Mikael's childhood. Her gleaming bronze hair was partly covered by an immaculate white fur hat in the Russian style.

And as she turned, her face came into view and Sophie gasped. There was no doubt—it was Elsa Blix!

The woman was moving quite purposefully in their direction, the pack of gentlemen in suits following in her wake.

"This trip has been a complete waste of time," she announced in English.

Her eyes passed over Sophie, then came to rest on Mikael. She looked him up and down, then said, "I wonder if something might be found to make it worth my while. . . ."

There was no doubt Elsa Blix was a strikingly good-looking woman—a strikingly good-looking woman with a pronounced interest in Mikael, who stepped forward now and shook Elsa Blix's hand with an eagerness that made Sophie feel bitter and mean-spirited.

"Mikael Petersen, at your service," he said. He seemed almost hypnotized by the woman's nearness; the air was full of her scent, a strange, pure, cold fragrance like the taste of biting on a twig in the woods in winter.

Elsa Blix kept Mikael's hand in her own right hand and

raised her left one to brush his face, sweeping along the crest of his shoulder and the top part of his arm where he had been hurt in the attack.

"Yes," she murmured, "I see: most interesting, most convenient. Do I deduce that you were at a certain birthday party the other week?"

Now even some vestigial notion of politeness couldn't stop Sophie from staring.

Elsa Blix raised her left hand again, this time with her fingers drawn up into a loose fist so that the large colored stone on her ring finger was level with the bridge of Mikael's nose. His eyes took on a faraway look, and to Sophie's absolute dismay, as the Snow Queen—it was impossible not to think of her that way—moved her hand first to the right and then to the left, Mikael's head moved with it.

"Have you heard mention of my ice palace?" said Elsa Blix. Mikael was following her words intently; she let her hand fall to rest on his cheek. "I have made my home in Spitsbergen for some years now. You will find it pleasant there, despite the cold. The only danger is that you will find it so beautiful you will never want to leave. . . ."

Sophie coughed. She had to do something, and it was the only thing she could think of.

"Perhaps you, too, will come and visit me in Spitsbergen?" said Elsa Blix, turning to Sophie and smiling, her hoarse voice low enough that only Sophie could hear her.

"Never!" Sophie said. She was by now so upset and angry that she was ready to knock the woman's hand to her side and drag Mikael away from her, but Elsa Blix retracted her hand herself. She snapped her fingers, and Mikael shook his head like a wet spaniel, some modicum of awareness returning to his eyes.

Elsa Blix cocked her head at Sophie.

"Not even if I have something you want?" she asked Sophie, her voice unpleasantly insinuating.

"There is nothing I want so much that it would make me come to you," Sophie answered, though she felt the lie in her words: Elsa Blix could tell Sophie things about her parents known to nobody else alive.

"Really?" said Elsa Blix.

She snapped her fingers carelessly, then turned to the retinue of businessmen. They had been standing some meters off, in bewilderment and barely suppressed impatience, waiting for her to finish this mystifying colloquy.

She swept out of the museum, down the steps, and into her car, a magnificent white behemoth whose uniformed chauffeur stood to attention beside the passenger door at the back. When she had gotten into the car, he closed the door after her and saluted the group at the top of the stairs, then got into the driver's seat.

Sophie looked around for Mikael, but he had gone to get their things from the cloakroom. He appeared a moment later and flung Sophie's coat at her; he had already carelessly buttoned his own around him, though the buttons were out of step with the holes, giving him an asymmetrical, disheveled look. He had the sled under his arm and he strode past Sophie without a word.

She fought her way into her coat and scarf and ran after him. What on earth was he doing?

Now he was bending down behind the car's rear bumper; he had put the sled down on the ground and was fiddling with its tether. As Sophie watched, he tugged experimentally on the cord, then mounted both feet on the sled and hunched down in an aerodynamic position.

One of the men in suits was going down the steps to try to get Mikael away from the car. But the vehicle was already pulling out and away, towing Mikael behind on his little sled as its speed increased.

"Mikael!" Sophie shouted. "Come back!"

He lifted his hand to show he'd heard, but did not turn around to look, and a moment later he had vanished around the corner.

Mikael's bizarre departure struck Sophie as an absolute calamity. The only tiny grain of consolation she could find in the situation was that clearly the others, without knowing at all who she and Mikael were, shared her sense of the utter undesirability of this development.

The most senior-looking man in a suit had run out into the middle of the square in his dress shoes. He stood now with the slush and snow up almost to his knees, uttering words that Sophie could not understand, because they were Swedish, but which almost certainly meant something like, "What the *hell* just happened here?"

Temperamentally, Sophie might have chosen to endure the horror of Mikael's disappearance on her own rather than surrounded by perplexed but kindly businessmen. When she was upset, she preferred to inflict herself only on herself, as it were, enforcing a stringent emotional *cordon sanitaire* until the storm was over. But there were certainly benefits of a practical sort to having it happen this way.

Even once the gentlemen had taken Sophie behind the scenes and sat her down and begun asking questions, though, it was difficult to know what to say. She had no grounds, really, for asserting that Elsa Blix had just kidnapped Mikael. To all intents and purposes, he had gone with her quite willingly. Only Sophie's gut told her that Elsa Blix was the villain in the piece. What a strange coincidence, too, that just the person with whom Sophie had been hoping to talk about her parents should be conducting some kind of business with Alfred Nobel. . . .

None of the people she spoke to could make any sense

of the allusion to the attack on the Mansion of Honor, but it made Sophie wonder whether Miss Blix might have been able to hypnotize or even brainwash Mikael especially easily as a consequence of some agent to which he had been exposed that night. Just as some unknown natural immunity had protected Sophie from the initial effects suffered by Mikael, so she seemed relatively invulnerable to the force of a personality to which Mikael had shown himself deeply susceptible.

She had mentioned Niels Bohr early on, with a noticeably positive effect in terms of the quality of attention the men paid to her. There were three of them now: the senior gentleman—who had replaced his wet shoes with a pair of carpet slippers for whose impropriety he had several times apologized—and two quite young ones, one of whom had given Sophie a funny wink that made her feel she was among friends. But the name Arne Petersen, when she finally thought of saying it some interminable minutes into the conversation—Mikael could be *anywhere* by now!—was like a magic key.

"Arne Petersen!" the senior gentleman said, then conferred with the two others in a rapid burst of Swedish.

"Yes," said Sophie hurriedly, "Mikael is Arne's younger brother, and we have been staying at his lodgings—oh, please will you telephone him and see what can be done?"

They tried to put through a telephone call to Mr.

Petersen, only he could not be reached. Then they made a series of other phone calls, Sophie sitting all the while with a cup of coffee and an iced pastry she could not force down, though it looked very nice, and an awful sick feeling in the pit of her stomach.

She could almost *feel* Mikael traveling farther and farther away, as though they were attached by a stretch cord whose tensile strength was being tested to its utmost limit. If only it could twang him back to her!

When she asked them what Elsa Blix was doing at the Nobel Museum, the gentlemen said that she had been in town for a set of negotiations that had broken down, after several days of butting heads, when Elsa Blix flatly refused to talk to anyone other than Nobel himself. Told that his health would not permit it, she had chosen to withdraw from the conversation altogether.

Nobody said as much, but Sophie felt fairly certain that they harbored just as much suspicion and hostility toward Elsa Blix as Sophie did herself.

The trouble, it emerged, was that nobody could actually say what crime had been committed. Mikael was a minor, it was true, but of an age to be fully capable of making choices. Who was to say he had not followed Elsa Blix of his own free will? Because it had taken them a good half hour to sort out who was who and the basic facts about the situation, they had lost the chance—were such a thing even possible—of asking the police to set up some kind of roadblock to detain Elsa Blix before she could leave the city.

"Where do you think they have gone," Sophie asked timidly, "assuming Mikael is still with Miss Blix?"

The men looked at one another, and then the nicer of the two young men leaned forward and said, "Sophie, there is no way of knowing whether or not your friend is still with her, but to the best of our knowledge she was to be driven directly to an airstrip north of the city. Her private aeroplane had been precleared for takeoff. She made a telephone call from this very office to check that there were no delays; I put the call through for her and was able to hear every word. . . ."

"Her aeroplane, you say?" said Sophie, feeling a little sick.

"It is entirely possible," added the senior gentleman, exchanging looks with the others, "that she has taken the boy onto the plane with her."

"Where are they going?" Sophie asked.

"To Spitsbergen, unless her plans have changed."

"To Spitsbergen!"

When Arne finally telephoned, in response to one of the half a dozen frantic messages left for him anywhere his presence seemed even remotely likely, the chief businessman told him quite succinctly what had happened to Mikael. Sophie felt very relieved that she was not the one to have to explain, though she knew Arne in no sense considered her responsible for Mikael's safety; it was more the other way round.

When he asked to speak to her, she took the telephone receiver with a mix of relief and trepidation.

"Are you all right?" he said urgently.

"Yes, I think so—but, Arne, how are we going to get Mikael back?"

Arne's silence told her what she knew already, that it would not be simple or easy.

"Sophie, the first thing will be for me to take you to see Alfred Nobel," he said.

Even in her distress, Sophie felt a surge of frustration and anger that it should take something so dramatic as Mikael's disappearance to precipitate the long-awaited meeting with Nobel.

"What should I do right now, though?" she asked.

"The people at the museum will send you home in a taxi," Arne answered. "Tell Mrs. McGregor what happened, and ask her to help you pack. Don't wait up for me—it may be very late by the time I get home; I still have to visit several factories and confer with their managers about the new security precautions—but we will leave first thing in the morning for Nobel's estate in the archipelago."

He rang off without saying anything else of substance,

and the most junior businessman shepherded Sophie to another, much smaller office and made the call to the taxi company.

Almost the worst thing about telling Mrs. McGregor was the subsequent outpouring of her sympathy, which took the form of incessant and highly annoying offers of tea, biscuits, cake, etc., until Sophie finally snapped at her and told her to go away. Sophie was deeply impatient to talk to Arne again, but it had been clear from their telephone conversation that he did not expect to arrive before midnight at the earliest, and possibly rather later. She could not face trying to put a call through to Fru Petersen—Arne would have spoken to her by now anyway—so she began to sort through her possessions.

It seemed nearly impossible to travel light in northern climes during the winter. She put on as many clothes as she could fit over one another in layers, having decided it would be sensible to sleep in them—they might be leaving very early in the morning, after all—and packed her school satchel with a few essentials: her sponge bag, emptied of almost everything other than her toothbrush and tooth powder and a small flannel for emergency face washing; the leather wallet with her passport and other travel documents and bankbook, with a quite thick wad of bills in several currencies tucked inside the pages of the passport (she had left untouched the money Fru Petersen had sewn into the hem of her coat); a few pairs of clean underthings and a spare blouse.

That done, she contemplated the bicycle with its cat-carrying module. It had been so kind of Mikael and Niels Bohr to construct the arrangement, she hated to disassemble it—but she needed some way to carry Trismegistus, and she could not imagine a bicycle would have much utility on this particular journey.

Tris clearly knew something was up. He had been following Sophie around the room as she packed, and he even—to her very great surprise—climbed into the basket once she had detached it from the bicycle, sniffing in the corners as if to inspect his quarters and see if they would do.

She went to bed almost immediately after supper, but it was impossible to fall asleep. By the time the clock struck one, she felt completely alert and restless and exhausted. Finally she got up and crept down the hallway to Mr. Petersen's sitting room to see if he was back. There was still no sign of him.

Trismegistus had accompanied her, a singular comfort, and watched as she mused for a while over the solitary bookshelf to see if there might be something good to read. There were several crime novels in English, but it happened that Sophie had read them already, and almost everything else was in Danish or Swedish or French, the last of which Sophie supposed herself perfectly capable of picking her way through, but which would not be very enjoyable.

There was a Swedish thesaurus, which would do Sophie little good either, but the next book on the shelf caught her eye.

Tris leaped up onto the table below the shelf and gave a plaintive yowl, as if urging Sophie to get a move on.

It was a combined atlas and railway schedule, a traveler's guide to the Hanseatic states and Russia, and Sophie found herself looking up Spitsbergen in the index.

There was a private airstrip on the island, but it was rare for outsiders to be given permission to use it. More usually one would take the train to Kiruna and travel overland, then get an icebreaker from Trømso to the main port of Longyearbyen. The regulations concerning the airspace were very strict, with the whole region governed by an intricate set of treaties between the Russians, Norwegians, and Finns.

Elsa Blix had a huge head start, especially since she'd flown north rather than traveling overland. But Sophie would get there sooner or later, even if Arne and Mr. Nobel couldn't help her on her way. She thought she had enough money to pay for the train herself, in a worst-case scenario, and she would at least have Tris for company. He had settled himself onto the pages of the railway atlas, his rumbling purr sounding louder than ever in the quiet of the small hours. A traveling companion would be welcome, even if it were merely—she regarded him affectionately—an overfed black cat with a muscular build.

In the end she fell restlessly asleep around five in the morning, waking up a few hours later to the sound of Mrs. McGregor moving about the kitchen. Arne put his head around the door at half past seven to say that the car would come for them at nine and that there was plenty of time for Sophie to have a bath and eat breakfast. It might be the last hot water she got for a long time, she thought, repressing a shudder. She was not in favor of rustic travel, believing hot water to be one of the great benefits of civilized life and anyone who chose voluntarily to forgo it for more than a day or two in the way of pleasure rather than punishment possibly actually insane.

They met up in the hallway ten minutes before the car was expected. Arne looked Sophie up and down and nodded his approval, but only until his eyes fell to the basket.

"Sophie, you're not bringing the cat with you, are you?" he asked incredulously.

"Of course I'm bringing Tris!" Sophie said, staring at him. It had not even occurred to her that Arne would be surprised—Trismegistus went where Sophie went; everybody knew that.

"No!" said Arne. "It's wildly impractical. Wouldn't you

rather leave the creature here? He'll be perfectly safe—Mrs. McGregor will look after him, won't you?"

"Yes, indeed," said the landlady, who was looking worried. "It will be no trouble at all—I'm very fond of cats!"

It was true, Sophie knew. The landlady had cooked Tris a number of delicious fish meals even in the short time they'd been staying with her. But the cat had begun to meow, and Sophie held firm. She could not help contrasting Arne's manner unfavorably with his brother's—Mikael had grumbled often enough about Tris, but in reality his approach to the cat had been something more like cheerful resignation, and in fact it was thanks to Mikael that Tris had even come with them from Scotland in the first place.

"Oh, all right," Arne said irritably, looking at his watch. "Is he going to keep up that racket in the car, though?"

Sophie leaned over to look in through the mesh at the end of the basket. She clucked to Tris, who settled down on his haunches and fell silent. She breathed a word of thanks.

Just then the car honked outside, and they scrambled down the stairs and into the backseat of a spacious black chauffeured limousine.

"It'll be a few hours of driving, Sophie," Arne said. "Nobel's house lies at the outer rim of the Stockholm archipelago, and though we will not need to take a ferry, the roads narrow as we go farther out of the city and we will sometimes need to stop at a bridge. You might try to get a bit more sleep, if you can."

"Oh, I can never sleep in cars," Sophie said. She settled into the corner and leaned her head against the window, tucking an arm protectively over Tris's basket and closing her eyes, which felt grainy and dry. Despite her words, she drifted off almost at once, her dreams a strange muddle of Great-aunt Tabitha and Alfred Nobel courting and war planes dropping bombs and Mikael's ghostly figure separated from her by an immense gulf of ice lit from beneath by flames.

The next thing Sophie knew, they were drawing into a grand driveway and up to an enormous house. Really, it looked more like a palace!

She was still so tired and worried that the first hour passed in a blur. Arne said that they would see Nobel after lunch, which would be brought to Sophie on a tray in her room so that she could rest. A silent uniformed servitor showed her to a lovely guest bedroom with its own private bathroom, and Sophie very gratefully washed her face and let Tris out onto the little balcony to stretch his legs. She lay down on top of the spotless white coverlet, but she had slept for long enough in the car that rest eluded her now.

She could think only of Mikael. Would Alfred Nobel help her and Arne get him back? The matter of Sophie's parents suddenly seemed quite secondary—and yet this might be the only time she ever had access to Nobel in person. She must keep everything in her head; the mere thought of forgetting something important made her heart race and her chest feel tight and constricted. She took a few deep breaths and tried to relax her muscles, but she could feel her hands reverting almost at once to tight bunched fists, and her buttocks were clenched.

When a knock came at the door, Sophie sprang guiltily back upright: one somehow felt a transgressor lying down fully clothed in the middle of the day on a bed in a stranger's house.

But it was only a maid bringing her a beautiful little lunch tray: open-faced smoked-salmon sandwiches on soft brown bread, a miniature tureen of leek-and-potato soup, a bowl of berries and yogurt, and a little plate with two iced petits fours that were so much exactly what Sophie liked that she experienced a sudden fit of paranoia. Had this visit been planned down to the smallest detail?

She felt quite a bit saner once she had eaten everything and drunk the pot of tea that accompanied the meal. She draped the snowy cloth napkin over the empty dishes and set the tray outside her door. She thought she would just lie down for a moment, Trismegistus tucking himself by her side in a tight, comforting ball, but the next thing she knew Arne was saying her name and she was struggling to rouse herself from deep sleep.

She frowned and rubbed her eyes. Looking at her watch, she saw it was after two o'clock.

"Mr. Nobel will see us in a few minutes," Arne said. "You will perhaps want to freshen up first? I'll wait for you on the landing; come and find me when you're ready, and we'll walk over to the other wing of the house together."

Sophie quickly brushed her teeth and washed her face with a flannel dipped in very hot water. The enormous tub, with its lavish supply of sea sponges and soaps and brightly colored bottles of scented elixirs and fluffy bath towels, elicited a longing glance. But a hurried bath was not a worthwhile bath, in Sophie's book, though she would not turn down the opportunity to have a really leisurely one if there were time later on. She combed her hair and scrunched up her nose at her face in the mirror, then took a few deep breaths and went to find Arne in the hall.

They walked down the main staircase and along a sort of gallery with spacious rooms on either side of it. They came to a green baize door, and Arne took a set of keys from his pocket and inserted one of them into the lock.

He paused before turning the doorknob.

"Sophie?" he said.

"Yes?"

"I should have said something sooner—do not be alarmed

when you see Mr. Nobel. His appearance is . . . well, let us say *unusual*—but he retains a very warm concern for you and your doings, and he has already promised me that he will do everything in his power to help us find Mikael and bring him home again."

The hallway on the other side of the door was plainer than the front part of the house, almost institutional in its fittings. Sophie could not help thinking of IRYLNS; there was even the same sort of vaguely medicinal smell in the air, the astringent scents of disinfectant and surgical dressings.

Arne led her past several closed doors to one that stood ajar. He pushed it the rest of the way open and motioned to Sophie to follow him.

It was a large room, the floor-to-ceiling windows covered by heavy navy-blue drapes. The room was dimly lit, with pieces of medical equipment standing in the corner, but Sophie's eyes were strongly drawn to the figure in the middle of the room. The body lay suspended horizontally in something that was more like a shallow fish tank than a hospital bed. The man had no clothes on, other than a sort of cloth covering his private parts; through the glass sides of the container could be seen the slight undulation of white limbs in the bright blue liquid medium (Sophie could not tell if it were more watery or gelatinous) that covered his entire body, with only the face projecting above the liquid surface.

A host of tubes was connected to all the parts of the body, but the strangest thing was what had been done to the head. Sophie was so fascinated by the mechanics that she did not feel even a twinge of the revulsion she might have expected. The man's neck and shoulders were held in place by a mechanical frame, his face visible over a cone-shaped collar rather like the ones worn in Shakespeare's day. But the whole top part of his skull had been cut away, and the flap of scalp folded over the edge of the bone; over his head was a protective dome-shaped plastic bubble through which could be seen the delicate folds of the brain within. It was interpenetrated with the filaments of a sort of net, wires running out of it to an elaborate machine that presumably regulated the electrical impulses in the gray matter.

A nurse sat on a stool beside the tank and periodically opened a window in the dome to dab the saliva from the corner of the man's mouth. The face beneath the glass was motionless.

"Mr. Nobel," Arne said, stepping forward not in the direction of the bed as such but toward the machines beside it, which Sophie now saw included a device along the lines of an old-fashioned ear trumpet as well as a pair of gramophone speakers.

Crackling emerged from the speakers.

"Is that Arne?"

The words came in a sort of whisper, hardly louder than

the susurration of leaves on a breezy evening. Arne moved closer to the equipment and fiddled with a dial.

"Yes, it's Arne Petersen," he said calmly as he tinkered. "I've brought Sophie Hunter to see you, Mr. Nobel; she's standing right here beside me. Sophie, will you say hello to Mr. Nobel? He can't see you, but with mechanical augmentation, his hearing is much better than that of an ordinary human being, and his English is also exceedingly good. He will be able to hear and understand everything you say. Do not be fooled by the lack of expression in his facial muscles—they are paralyzed, and the technology serves only to amplify the small amount of movement he retains in the mouth and throat."

"Sophie," said the disembodied voice from the speakers. "Welcome."

She stared at the body lying before her. The first thing that came to her mind was the impossibility of imagining it, albeit in a younger and healthier incarnation, in naked proximity to Tabitha's. But the face was unmistakably that of the man in the photograph. This was Sophie's grandfather, incomprehensible as the notion might seem!

About to speak, she stopped herself and cast a glance at Arne, who said quietly, "I am here exclusively as an intermediary. You will let me know if I can facilitate communications in any way, but I do not consider myself properly a party to the conversation—I am bound by as strong an obligation of confidentiality as the priest in his confessional. The nurse must remain, but I promise you she speaks no English. What is said here will remain within these four walls."

"Sophie," the voice said again, this time more urgently. "I learned of Tabitha's death only a few days ago—did she leave you a letter?"

"She left me a letter," Sophie said somberly, casting another glance at Arne and wondering whether he really would understand the importance of keeping Tabitha's secret. "A letter, a birth certificate, and a pair of photographs."

"I have seen the birth certificate," said the voice; the face above the collar was absolutely remote and impassive, as though it had been carved from marble. "I can imagine, at the very least, what the letter may have said. What were the photographs?"

"One was a picture of two young people, a photograph taken in San Remo in the 1890s."

The sound might have been nothing more than a glitch in the amplification, but Sophie couldn't help interpreting it as a sigh.

"The other picture," she continued, "was a photograph of my parents in the company of Elsa Blix."

"Elsa Blix!" Arne exclaimed. "But how can this be? Elsa Blix is the one who's taken Mikael—what does that have to do with this bit of ancient history, if you will forgive my calling it that? However much it may matter to Sophie to find out what happened to her parents, Mikael's safety is far more important."

"Elsa Blix used to work with my father," Sophie said.

"In one sense," said the remote voice belonging to the man in the bed, "the fact of Sophie and Mikael's happening to encounter Elsa Blix falls under the heading of the one-in-a-million coincidence. In another, their convergence at the Nobel building in Stockholm results from a rationally comprehensible set of pressures that make it not nearly so surprising. I do not know precisely why Sophie and Mikael found themselves there, though the onset of war had, of course, brought them inexorably to neutral Sweden, and it was a very natural thing for them to find themselves at the doorstep of a building to which they might be expected to feel some connection. And I have, after all, taken considerable trouble to render the museum attractive to members of the general public. Elsa Blix was there because she had been trying to sell me something: namely, the plans of the device built by Sophie's father."

"But—"

"What—"

Sophie and Arne had spoken at the same time; Arne fell quiet, and motioned to Sophie to continue.

"Your brother's disappearance," said Nobel, "may be no

more than a random act of malice. But when Niels Bohr alerted me several weeks ago to Sophie's wish to explore the old connection between Blix and her parents, I knew nothing good would come of it!"

"Who is Elsa Blix, then?" Sophie asked. "I mean, who is she really? I know she studied with Bohr—he told me she was a research scientist turned weapons dealer. I suppose she must have kept a copy of the plans after she left my father's factory. But why did she take Mikael, and how will we get him back? Does she really live in an ice palace in Spitsbergen, and will we have to go there to find him?"

"A woman of many questions, I gather," said Nobel.

Sophie was starting to be able . . . well, not to reconcile the voice with the uncanny shape in the tank, but at least to credit it with a full personality and consciousness. She found it made more sense to look in the direction of the speakers than to keep her eyes on that strange, cold face.

"I will tell you everything I can," Nobel continued. "It happens that I knew Elsa Blix's mother—a beautiful socialite, a butterfly flitting around Europe as whimsy took her. As a young girl, Elsa had a fierce intelligence that led her to feel something like contempt for her mother—and yet she herself had little more self-discipline than the mother she despised. I had known Elsa slightly when she was a child. Her mother and my wife were acquainted. I met her again at the institute at the end of her fellowship period—she interviewed for a job with one of my companies, and I interviewed her myself, once she had been thoroughly vetted by the personnel department, to see whether she would be a suitable member of Alan Hunter's staff in Russia. Her technical expertise complemented his nicely, and he had a high opinion of her brains from the time they'd spent together at the institute; I thought a productive dynamic might arise between the two of them."

"And did it?" Sophie asked. It was mad to linger on the distant past when Mikael even now might be in pressing danger—time now mattered in hours or even seconds rather than years and decades—but the past also seemed to hold the secrets of Elsa Blix's present motivation, and Sophie supposed it might be worth taking the extra time to find out what she could.

"Yes and no," said Nobel, and Sophie thought it might have been another sigh that issued from the machines. "Alan and Elsa did work well together; she contributed a fair amount to the technical specifications, though not, perhaps, as much as your mother did, Sophie. Rose was a quieter woman than Elsa, which led to her being often underestimated."

"You speak as if you knew them all quite well!" said Sophie, slightly bewildered.

"I take an interest in all those who work for me," said

Nobel, "but Alan Hunter's project was particularly dear to me. I was already quite an elderly man, of course, but I was not the pitiful wrecked carcass you see before you now. I traveled twice to see the factory, and was intimately involved with your father's plans. He was, after all—Arne, you will pretend you did not hear this part—my only son. And the device he hoped to build was the weapon I had always dreamed of: an explosive device powered by a nuclear reaction so powerful and so profoundly destructive that the mere threat of its use, or so I then believed, promised to end conventional warfare forever.

"During my first visit, I truly believed the dream was at long last about to come to fruition. The project was going well, with the unmistakable aura of a prosperous and productive workplace. Your father was a very talented manager, above and beyond his intellectual gifts, and both the engineering staff and the manual laborers in the factory seemed devoted to him personally as well as to the project. Of course, there were significant financial incentives for them to stay on or ahead of schedule. Your father would have received a substantial bonus—a mix of company stock and hard cash in a currency of his choice—for early completion."

"Was he still on track for that when the factory blew up?" Sophie asked, trying to listen for what Nobel was omitting and ask the right questions to bring it out.

"He was not," Nobel said. "On my second and final visit, which took place about two months before the explosion, I found a singularly different environment. A series of small but troublesome acts of industrial sabotage had time and again halted the production line. This in itself would not have been catastrophic, but it had a sort of cascade effect. The factory workers—untutored peasants!—had become convinced the project was cursed. Their superstition and ignorance were such that this was no metaphor. A number of men had left already, and the village priest was agitating against the project in a way that it made it difficult for your father to recruit new workers. The worries heaped on his shoulders had pushed him dangerously close to the brink of absolute exhaustion."

"What about Elsa Blix?" Sophie asked. "Was she still there? Tabitha said in her letter that she left a month or so before it all came to an end, but she could not tell me how or why the rift came about."

"She was still there when I visited," Nobel said, "although the professional relationship was in the final stages of its decay. It had become clear, over the life of the project, that the superficial alignment of goals between your father and Elsa Blix was just that—a matter of surfaces only. Alan shared the dream that has united me and Niels Bohr and Tabitha Hunter over these many years—a dream of universal peace.

Elsa had quite another idea, and I think your father had almost come to see her as a demonic force: she hoped to persuade him to break his contract with me, in defiance of the requirements both of honor and of his deepest ideals."

"Why would she want him to break the contract?" Sophie asked.

"So that they could sell the weapon—the atom bomb, as they called it amongst themselves—to the highest bidder. Elsa had a vision of her own, and it was not a vision of perpetual peace. . . ."

"My father wouldn't have broken his word to you, would he?" Sophie asked anxiously, aware of the unlikelihood of getting an unbiased answer and yet quite unable to stop herself from asking.

"He refused to break the contract," Nobel answered, "and he recoiled in horror at the notion of the weapon's being put on the open market. The force of the weapon was literally inconceivable—the devastation it was projected to wreak was beyond the capabilities of the human imagination to grasp."

"What did Elsa Blix do, then, once she realized my father really meant it when he said no?"

"On the face of it," said Nobel, "the answer is simple. She resigned her position and took a new job working for a massive German munitions company, though her tenure there was brief. Certain instabilities in her personality made it difficult, I think, for her to work well with others, especially with administrative superiors of whose intelligence she had a low opinion. The original psychometric testing we did before we hired her had shown as much, but I chose to overlook those results—subsequent events proved the error of my decision."

"On the face of it, yes, I see," Sophie said slowly. "But what do you think really happened?"

"At the time, I thought nothing more than that I had made a poor hire," Nobel said.

Arne had remained silent, but was following the conversation's revelations with a bewildered intentness that made Sophie suddenly feel, with her heart rather than her head, that Arne might be even more worried about Mikael than Sophie was.

"Elsa Blix was a failed experiment, a former employee who'd left on rancorous terms," Nobel continued, "but little more than that. For many years, I believed that the mystery of your parents' death would never be solved. The initial investigation went nowhere. The disaffected worker whom the other employees suspected of having committed the earlier acts of sabotage, and who may well have detonated the charge that blew the factory up, was found dead a week later at the bottom of a nearby quarry, having gone over the edge after a bout of solitary drinking, but it is also possible the accident's real instigator decided to tie up the last remaining loose end by getting rid of him."

"So?" Sophie said impatiently. Arne put out his hand as if to restrain her, then drew it back without actually touching her. "What happened to make you question that version of events?"

"Arne may speak to this more directly than I," said Nobel.

Sophie looked at Arne, who shrugged.

"Part of it you know already," he said. "You remember the day I practically dropped dead of shock at the sight of that page that appeared in the pantelegraph machine at your old school. . . ."

"Of course," said Sophie.

"When I saw you last in København, I told you that those images represented work we thought had perished with your father," Arne continued. "I sent them immediately to Nobel—they represented only a small fraction of the full plans, of course, but their very existence gave us reason to believe that the rest of the plans might have survived as well."

"Who sent them, though?" Sophie asked urgently. "Where did they come from?"

"It is truly an unsolved mystery how that page turned up in my classroom," Arne said. "Why, the machines were connected only to each other—there was no line to the outside world! I suspected an illusion or a piece of trickery of some sort, but could not work out how such a thing would have been pulled off; for a while, I even came to suspect that occult forces might have been at work."

This did not seem entirely far-fetched to Sophie. It had been a summer of paranormal manifestations in all aspects of her life—it seemed as likely to her that the plans had been transmitted by someone dead as by someone alive, though she was not sure who that person could have been.

"I set out to inquire, on my employer's behalf, of course, as to where the rest of the plans might be," Arne continued. "The path led straight to Elsa Blix."

"What do you mean?" Sophie asked.

Arne looked at his watch.

"In about ten minutes," he said, "we will have a conversation with the woman herself. We can hope that some of these matters will be clarified then. In the meantime, I will just say that as we put the message out that we'd be interested in purchasing more pages, should any such thing exist, the word *Spitsbergen* first came to be mentioned. Not long afterward, Mr. Nobel received a direct communication from Blix herself. She had the plans, she said; they were missing certain crucial elements to do with the actual fuel the device would require, elements she had tried in vain to reconstruct, and partly as a result of this she would consider selling the plans to Nobel Enterprises, if the price was right."

"Would you buy them from her?" Sophie asked anxiously.

"I meant to," Nobel said. "She has been in Stockholm this past week meeting with my people and trying to hammer out a deal. But Bohr's latest work has changed the terms of the conversation. With the recent discovery made by Frisch and Meitner, this problem of the fuel has to a great extent been solved, which means that the weapon teeters on the edge of becoming a reality—the plans are infinitely more valuable than they would have been mere months ago. Infinitely more valuable—and infinitely more dangerous!"

"But why would she have waited so many years to try to sell the plans to you?" Sophie asked, quite confused.

"That, Sophie, is the question," Nobel said, the voice sounding heavier, wearier than before. "I have often felt, over the years, as though some shadowy adversary were thwarting me."

"An adversary?"

"One wonders, of course, whether it might not be a paranoid fantasy," Nobel continued. "A factory closure in Libya, a lost convoy of merchandise in the Great Lakes, a valued employee poached, or a contract lost to a competitor—why should any one of these things be connected to another?

Might it not be a flaw of the human meaning-generating system to find patterns in events that may really and truly be unrelated?"

"You think it wasn't just a fantasy, though," Sophie said.

"I became increasingly convinced that a single person's diabolical scheming could be seen operating against me," Nobel answered, "and that it could only be an individual whose ambition saw no limits—someone who imagined that the era of Nobel was passing, and that a vacancy would be created thereby for a new master of life and death."

The voice fell silent. It had become weaker and threadier, and the nurse seemed to know that something was needed, for she opened the dome again—Sophie had a sudden comic-grotesque revelation that it worked exactly like the sliding cover on a hot dish at a catered dinner—pulled back Nobel's lips with her fingers, and sponged off the inside of his mouth with a carbohydrate solution, then adjusted several settings on the machine regulating the flow of nutrients into his body.

"This person clearly intended," continued Nobel, sounding stronger again now, though Arne was looking worried, "to capture an even larger share of the market for munitions than I had—and this person did not share my way of thinking about weapons as deterrents to violence, but instead gloried in their use."

"Why do you think this person must be Elsa Blix, though?" Sophie persisted.

"Here is Elsa Blix with the plans seemingly in her possession—she certainly showed my representatives enough pages to convince me the claim was true—and an offer on the table. She would give me the missing bits, she said, in return for my concession of a massive tranche of shares in various companies I control. My companies are structured in a relatively unusual fashion, beyond most people's understanding or knowledge, but this offer showed an exceptional grasp of the corporate governance structures—in other words, of exactly which holdings would give their possessor the most control throughout my empire."

"Do you think she took the plans with her long ago when she left the factory?" Sophie asked.

"I think something much worse than that. I have come to believe it may have been Blix herself who instigated the explosion. I suspect that she was behind the sabotage at the factory. I believe that after she had gone, she continued to maneuver behind the scenes to pressure your father into changing his mind about selling the weapon to another purchaser, one who had actual intentions of using it. And I believe that when it finally dawned on her that your father was not going to budge, she took more drastic measures. If the weapon could not be possessed by those she thought deserved it, neither would it come into my ownership—and she resolved to blow the factory to kingdom come."

"But what basis do you have for saying this?" Sophie cried out. In some ways, she wanted it very badly to be true—it was awful, but it would at least make sense of her parents' deaths. "Have you any evidence? It could perfectly well be pure speculation!"

"The matter cannot be resolved on the basis of the information currently in my possession," Nobel admitted. "To return to the developments of recent days, it became clear that negotiations would not reach a successful conclusion. Blix was frustrated that I was not there myself—she made my presence a new condition of continuing to treat with me. I was unwilling to invite a hostile stranger to contemplate my present condition of physical weakness, so that was not an option, but though I insisted that the group of executives in Stockholm was empowered to negotiate on my behalf, the conversation broke down on the third day. At the time she encountered you and Mikael, Sophie, she had already announced the cancellation of any intention to hand over the plans."

"But why has she taken Mikael?" Sophie exclaimed. This elaborate account did not offer any enlightenment. "What can she want with him?"

"This, we will ask the lady herself," Arne said, tapping his watch and going over to make a few adjustments on a machine Sophie hadn't especially singled out, full as the room was with all sorts of medical equipment. She now saw the typewriter-like apparatus of an old-fashioned teletype, and a moment later the humming began that signaled transmission of a message over the lines.

The words appeared letter by letter on a screen that was large enough for Sophie to read, and that seemed to feed directly into Nobel's sensory equipment, because he spoke in response to the sentences that appeared, and the machine itself transcribed his words.

NOBEL, ARE YOU READY TO MEET ME FACE-TO-FACE?

IMPOSSIBLE.

THEN THERE IS NO TREATING WITH YOU.

ON THE CONTRARY. I HAVE FOUND AN EMISSARY TO SEND ON MY BEHALF, ONE ON WHOM I BESTOW ALL OF MY OWN AUTHORITY TO NEGOTIATE.

I ALREADY MET WITH YOUR MINIONS IN STOCKHOLM. I HAVE NO INTEREST IN PROXIES.

THIS IS DIFFERENT.

HOW?

I AM SENDING YOU MY GRANDDAUGHTER.

The pause that followed was long enough that Sophie started to wonder whether the machine was still working. After almost a minute, the letters began appearing again.

YOU DO NOT HAVE A GRANDDAUGHTER.

I HAVE A GRANDDAUGHTER. HER NAME IS SOPHIE HUNTER. SHE WAS THE ONLY SURVIVOR OF THE RUSSIAN ACCIDENT THAT KILLED ALAN AND ROSE HUNTER; SHE IS THEIR ONLY CHILD.

SOPHIE HUNTER—BUT ALAN HUNTER . . . DOES THAT MEAN HE WAS YOUR SON?

I AM NO LIAR.

Another pause ensued, and then the words began again.

SEND HER TO ME.

WILL YOU PROMISE TO KEEP HER SAFE?

I WILL NOT HARM HER.

SHE WILL DISCUSS THE MATTER OF HER FATHER'S WORK WITH YOU, BUT THERE IS ANOTHER THING THAT CONCERNS US: THE BOY YOU TOOK FROM STOCKHOLM.

THE BOY?

THE BOY IS SOPHIE'S FRIEND, AND THE BROTHER OF MY CLOSE ASSOCIATE ARNE PETERSEN.

HOW AMUSING! WAS THAT SOPHIE, THEN, THAT SLIM LITTLE DARK-HAIRED THING IN THE MUSEUM LOBBY? I WILL NOT PREVENT HER FROM SEEING THE BOY, BUT IT WILL BE UP TO HIM WHETHER HE WANTS TO GO AWAY WITH HER AGAIN.

ARNE WILL ACCOMPANY SOPHIE ON HER TRAVELS.

NO! I WILL RECEIVE SOPHIE, AND SOPHIE ALONE. ASSUMING SHE CAN GET AS FAR AS LONGYEARBYEN, I WILL SEND SOMEONE TO GUIDE HER THE REST OF THE WAY.

IT IS TOO DANGEROUS! YOU CANNOT EXPECT SUCH A YOUNG GIRL TO TRAVEL ALONE.

SHE WILL DO PERFECTLY WELL; YOU MAY RETAIN SOME LOCAL AGENT TO ACCOMPANY HER FOR SOME PART OF THE WAY, BUT DO NOT DARE SEND ONE OF YOUR CLOSE ASSOCIATES WITH HER, NOBEL! WE DO NOT LIKE OUTSIDERS IN THIS PART OF THE WORLD. I WILL AWAIT HER ARRIVAL WITH INTEREST.

And that was that—Nobel essayed several more remarks, but they met with no response, and at last Arne turned off the machine and said that they would get no more from Elsa Blix today.

"Of course you won't let Sophie go," he added.

"Of course I must go," Sophie said, "even if it is dangerous!"

"Sophie must go," said Nobel. "Arne, you will find someone local who can travel with her for part of the way; I leave the arrangements solely in your hands."

"Mr. Nobel," Sophie said tentatively, "are you really willing to have me negotiate on your behalf? How will I know what to say?"

"I believe I have no choice," said Nobel. "Arne, I must rest. Will you escort Sophie back to her room, and ensure she is provided with all the creature comforts? Sophie, you will forgive me if I do not see you again before you leave. I must marshal my resources very carefully, and I have tapped into them more deeply already than is advisable. Your train leaves late tonight."

"My train?"

"The first leg of your journey involves a train from here to Kiruna," Arne said, standing up and offering Sophie his arm, which he would never usually have done but which seemed a function of the strangely courtly atmosphere created by Nobel's manner of speaking.

"One thing more," the voice said.

Arne and Sophie halted.

"This is no time for me to make you a serious offer. The question of Mikael's safety will weigh heavily on your mind. But, Sophie, you must know that I consider you my heir. I have long since been prepared for death; only the snares of worldly ambition tied me to life in this body. Most of all, the atom bomb has seemed to me a piece of unfinished business. If I can close the books on that, I will be ready at long last to depart from this earth. I cannot do it without you. And in exchange for this assistance, and in recognition of the relationship between us, I have written you into my will as sole—"

"Stop!" Sophie said, covering her ears and shrinking away from the voice. "It's too much! I don't want it!"

"I knew it was the wrong time," Nobel said, the voice little more than a whisper now. "Safe travels, Sophie. It is impossible to say whether we will meet again, but please believe me when I say you will be very much in my thoughts."

As they traveled back the way they'd come, Arne stayed far enough ahead of Sophie that she had to struggle to keep up with him.

"Go slower!" she said, panting. They were practically running down the hall. He slowed down and turned to look at her.

"Are you angry with me?" she asked.

Arne did not deny it.

"It's stupid, I know," he said, sounding almost hopeless. "You will do everything you can to find Mikael and bring him back. But I thought I would be the one to go—how will I stand waiting to know the outcome?"

They had come to a small sitting room, and Arne rang a bell and asked the maid to bring them tea and biscuits. Once these had been set out on the table and the maid dismissed, Arne began laying out the practical arrangements concerning the train to Kiruna and how Sophie would proceed from there.

"Must I really travel alone?" she said. "Couldn't you come with me?"

"I wish I could, Sophie," Arne said earnestly. "It doesn't

sit at all right with me to send you off like this! But Elsa Blix is a woman of her word—if she wants you to come on your own, we must see that it happens that way. In a strange sense, she is almost a trustworthy character—violent, malevolent perhaps, but not, in my estimation, actively deceitful. And we will not be sending you without guidance—Nobel has a man in the north who will meet you at the station in Kiruna and help you to the next stage of your journey."

"How long will it take me altogether?" Sophie asked.

"That, I cannot say, but I would guess it may take you some weeks—certainly the trip is more likely to be measured in weeks than in days."

"Weeks!" Sophie said, staring at him. She had still imagined that she might be in Spitsbergen within forty-eight hours, but she supposed that traveling overland would be very slow. "But, Arne—how do we know that Mikael will still be all right?"

"We can't know," he said. "We can only hope."

The same car they'd ridden in that morning—it seemed a lifetime ago—took Sophie to the train station. Arne sat in the back with Sophie and Tris; the chauffeur had been so silent and uncommunicative all day that Sophie wondered whether he was not a deaf-mute.

The station was on the main line north of Stockholm.

Getting on there meant a slower trip, Arne had said, but it wasn't worth going all the way back into the city to secure a place on the express.

There were only two platforms, north and south, and a small waiting room with a news kiosk, where Arne bought Sophie some sweets and magazines for the journey. It was strange not seeing any of the familiar kinds of chocolate and boiled sweets and packets of toffee that one would have bought in Scotland—the case could certainly be made that Scandinavian candies were as nice as Scottish ones, but their niceness was partially canceled out by the lack of familiarity.

When the train pulled into the station, Arne helped Sophie up the steps and tipped the conductor to make sure she got safely to the sleeper berth that had been booked for her. It was a bit of a scramble sorting herself out, and the train was pulling out of the station by the time Sophie had found a spot at the window in the corridor and looked out to see if she could wave good-bye.

Part 3

October–December 1938

The Stockholm Archipelago

and Points North

The railway journey felt longer than Sophie could have possibly imagined, though she experienced a strangely stirring moment when they pulled into a station that really was just a perfectly ordinary little fortified frontier town—the only people visible on the platform were a handful of soldiers—and saw an actual sign on one of the platforms that said POLCERKELN, with an arrow pointing north toward the Arctic Circle. It was the idea of north!

She had already come so far that the daylight hours were severely truncated. Well away by now from the highly populated region at the southern end of the Scandinavian peninsula, the train wound its way through the pristine white landscape like a steam serpent, the regular chugging of the engine lulling Sophie into a rhythmic stupor much like sleep.

At Kiruna, after roughly twenty hours of train travel, Sophie would leave her things at the station hotel, booking a room for the night, and then proceed in a taxi to the photographic studio where she would find her guide for the next leg of the trip. Arne had made a string of telephone calls and roped in on Sophie's behalf a longtime agent of Nobel, whose tentacles seemed to reach even to the most remote parts of the globe.

Kiruna was hellish: not hellish in a trivial sense, but hellish like Pandemonium in *Paradise Lost*. At the station hotel, Sophie followed instructions, taking a room and dropping off her luggage and setting Tris up with a rigged litter pan and small bowls of food and water. It was a perfectly civilized hotel, but through the window could be seen an industrial landscape of extraordinarily grim ugliness. Sophie learned from the chambermaid that Lapps had mined here for centuries, long before Sweden claimed sovereignty and built the town up into its present state. The smelting furnaces, the electric power stations, the mountain of iron ore two hundred and fifty feet high that stood directly across from the hotel—evidence of the mines was everywhere.

The photographer Johan Turi had been primed by Arne

with news of Sophie's arrival. He had already prepared an inventory of gear and clothing, and another one of provisions, both of which he offered for her perusal.

Looking at the lists made Sophie feel somewhat helpless. She strongly disliked shopping, and had no idea where to start—it was already dark again, and she devoutly hoped to be off the next morning. But Turi explained that his studio served as a kind of expeditionary outfitter as well, and that everything she needed would be found in the storeroom and billed to Nobel's account.

He opened up a door to reveal an utterly fantastic treasure house of delights. Sophie was especially taken with the notion that they would bring with them tins of Mediterranean sardines and Californian asparagus as well as big blocks of chocolate and nougat and a whole round of cheese in a red wax rind.

The only worry was boots—he did not have any in a small enough size for Sophie, but they agreed that her current ones would do for now, and that she would almost certainly be able to purchase a warmer pair made of reindeer fur from one of the tribes with whom they would later travel.

He brushed off Sophie's worries about the logistics of transporting Tris.

"It is certainly more common to travel with a dog than a cat," he said easily, "but I see no reason why it should pose any special difficulties. I will have to count his weight as part of your luggage and charge accordingly, though!"

The things Sophie had bought would be sent over to the hotel, so that she could integrate her other possessions into the load, and they would set out the next morning at six. She felt that perhaps she would not mention to Trismegistus that he was yet again being categorized under the dreaded rubric of *luggage*.

When she came back out into the street, she was startled to find it almost as bright as real day—brighter!—the electric lights throughout town making for a striking spectacle. Sophie supposed that the prevalence of power plants must make it quite cheap to do this. In every other respect, though, it seemed massively out of keeping with the town's ugly utilitarian aesthetic.

Back at the hotel, Sophie sent a brief telegram to Arne, but there was little to say beyond the fact that she had arrived safely and found Turi without any difficulty. Far too many days still stood between Sophie and the likelihood of actually seeing Mikael for her to make any promises—Arne would know that the success of her quest would depend on factors almost certainly beyond her control.

Sophie hated to think of there being such a thing as factors beyond her control—but facts must be faced!

She had not had the self-possession to inquire of the

photographer as to their mode of travel, he had so briskly taken the reins of the conversation and, in his pleasant way, steered Sophie to what was needed. But she learned the next morning that the first leg of their journey would be accomplished in a horse-drawn sleigh. Once they reached Karesuando, they would rendezvous with the group of Sami who would serve as their escorts for the next leg, from which point onward they would travel exclusively by reindeer!

Trismegistus had been singularly subdued on the train. Perhaps he understood that the limits of official tolerance for animals on the railway had better not be pressed too far. But as soon as they set out in the sleigh, a sustained low yowling began to issue from the basket. The noise was a trial to the nerves, even if one were fond of cats in general and Tris in particular. Turi said nothing at first, but he exchanged looks with the driver, a man of few words, and Sophie began to worry that steps would be taken.

After breakfast, Turi observed that as Tris sounded on Sophie's account to be a most unusual cat, perhaps it would be worth giving him an unusual degree of freedom and seeing if that suited him better than his cage-bound captivity.

"What if he runs away, though?" Sophie asked. Her dreams were always full of terrible moments where she could no longer find the place where she was supposed to be living and the problem would be compounded by Tris somehow being in her arms and on the verge of slipping out of her grasp and getting lost out in the world forever as Sophie helplessly watched him race away from her.

But Turi regarded her with a bracing kind of disappointment and said that sometimes one had to trust the other person to make good use of the freedom granted him, and that the chance the cat might run off was the price one paid for this. So when they got back into the sleigh and were moving again, Sophie released the catch on the carrier and waited to see what Tris would do.

For a few minutes, he stayed crouched in the bed of the basket, but then he cautiously sniffed his way out and tucked himself under the blanket on Sophie's lap. It was a thick felt rug that she had wrapped around herself from shoulders to feet, and his body felt warm against hers; she could feel his rumbling purr as they proceeded along what could scarcely be called a road.

They stopped regularly for meals and to sleep, usually hiring a few rooms or just a spot on the floor from some modest householder who would give them a meal and a place to lie down for the night. Not enough people traveled this way to support inns, but there was sometimes a hostel or even just a hut near the side of the road equipped with sleeping pallets and blankets and the facilities for heating water and food. In a town called Jukasjärvi they stayed with the minister and his wife, and Sophie marveled at the names written in the visitors' book in the green and red church. It was an imposing leather-bound volume that was already well over two hundred years old. Sophie signed her name only a few lines below those of the renowned balloonist and aeronaut Frank Hedges Butler and his daughter, and if one turned back to the book's first pages—it must have taken a great leap of faith, on the part of whoever had first set the ledger up, in the length of futurity for the gradual filling-in of visits few and far between—the names and dates soon spoke from the eighteenth century: the French scientist Maupertuis and his friend Celsius had been here in 1736, and the Swedish naturalist and classifier Linnaeus in 1732.

In summer, this part of the world was said to be extraordinarily beautiful. It was beautiful now, too, but in such a cold, frozen way that even the possibility of summer seemed inconceivable. Though at night, once they had built up the fire, they often found themselves almost inconveniently warm, it was far colder and darker here than the imagination could encompass. It did not become light until the late morning, so that much of their travel took place in full darkness or by the brightness of the moon on nights when there was one. Very soon there would be no daylight whatsoever.

They reached Karesuando, on the frozen river that separated Lapland from Russian Finland, and began the next leg of the trip to Trømso. The days of reindeer travel that followed were like something out of an amazing dream. They slept in reindeer sleeping bags covered by soft coverlets made of hare skin; the pillows were stuffed with reindeer hair instead of feathers. The tent they mostly stayed in at night was made of forked branches stuck in the ground in the shape of a triangle, the larch trunks lashed together with reindeer-hide cords. It had an inner framework like the ribs of an animal—Turi told Sophie a folktale about two children rescued from an evil spirit by a reindeer who turned its body into a living tent, with the ribs as the frame and the hide as the cover.

One night at supper—reindeer meat and berry jam on a sort of flatbread—Sophie was sitting and idly talking with Turi when something caught her eye. It was a small and roughly printed newssheet that must have come with the supplies they had bought several days earlier at a tiny trading outpost. It seemed to have been printed in Denmark, and it contained a column of smudged print reporting on the current—well, no longer, but it had been current a week earlier!—state of affairs at the institute in København!

Niels Bohr had been put under surveillance. His telephone was tapped, and the new government had attempted to trick him into incriminating himself in all sorts of ways. There was extensive sabotage in the bomb factories that had been taken over by the European Federation, with great loss of life, and the fighters in the resistance seemed to be trying to decide whether they should actually blow up the institute.

It was amazing to think that this piece of newspaper even existed, let alone of its having traveled so far. Sophie hoped desperately that Bohr and the others were all right. When would she see them again? Almost certainly not for a very long time—not if Europe and the Hanseatic states toppled over into full-blown war.

When they reached Trømso, Sophie took her leave of the group. It had seemed an eternity of travel; it was an extraordinary thing to reenter the modern world after this spell of a life that did not materially differ—other than in the peripheral existence of things like tinned food—from how one might have lived in the eighteenth century. She had an unpleasant sense of a safe interlude having concluded, and of returning once more to the dangerous space of Elsa Blix's surveillance.

Remembering the instructions about traveling alone, she took a very cold leave of Turi and followed the next bit of Arne's directions, which involved Sophie finding the local telegraph office and notifying Elsa Blix of the details of her arrival in Spitsbergen, where she would be met. The ship to Longyearbyen, Spitsbergen's main port, left only once a week. It was a special icebreaker—an ordinary ship might not have been able to make the crossing safely at this time of year—and the trip was rough. Sophie was sick a few times into a bucket on deck, and regretted the fact of there being no regular ferry service—a larger ship might have been less likely to tip her over the edge into active illness, though some level of queasiness on this sort of a journey seemed a depressing inevitability.

Tris had proved himself so thoroughly capable of dog-type companionship that she had given up any pretense of containing him in a box or basket. The cat tailed Sophie wherever she went, and found himself a nice warm spot on the ship near the tea samovar; Sophie was impressed at his ability to extract milk from the otherwise fairly hard-hearted cook in the tiny galley.

In a way Sophie was grateful for the seasickness. It stopped her from thinking so obsessively about whether she would find Mikael, and in what condition; what Elsa Blix wanted from Nobel; and whether Sophie would be able to persuade Blix to divulge more about Sophie's parents. There seemed a significant element of personal danger, but that Sophie largely disregarded. If she couldn't do anything for Mikael, she was not sure she would much care whether she lived or died. Also, being freezingly cold and extremely queasy was conducive to a stoical sort of detachment about one's personal survival.

The vehicle that had been sent to meet her in the port was a white sleigh drawn by four white horses, unmistakably the style of Elsa Blix. The driver did not ask to see Sophie's credentials—indeed, they had no common language, and he drove her in a silence that seemed increasingly ominous as they drew away from town. The horses strained to pull up the steep, mountainous road leading out of Longyearbyen, with only a handful of buildings interspersed through the landscape of rock, snow, and ice. Her stomach settled down a little as they drove, at least so long as she didn't look over the edge of the precipice.

As the palace of ice came into view, Sophie at first thought it must be a natural feature of the island; only gradually did she come to see it for what it was: the work of human hands. The drive seemed to take forever, and then suddenly there they were at the gates and the driver was letting her off and pulling away without asking whether she would prefer him to wait.

The gatehouse was set into a wall, a glistening updating of medieval-style fortification made out of some material that Sophie could not at all identify but that shared some of the properties of ice. Sophie knocked at the door with enormous trepidation.

The gatekeeper who answered it was small and wizened, so thoroughly bundled up in layers of reindeer fur that one could not discern whether she was skinny or round. She ushered Sophie through the little house and out through another door into a passageway that seemed to have been actually carved through the rock. One half expected it to be lit by torches, but in fact the dim greenish light was emitted from glass tubes that Sophie thought must be some variant of the Tesla lamps (filled with neon or argon) that had been a popular subject of experimentation back at the institute.

The woman led Sophie along as though she must understand very well where they were going and what was about to happen, though in fact Sophie felt utterly perplexed and bewildered. The environment seemed frighteningly remote and isolated, but not in any other obvious sense threatening; it was a palace with no populace, a desert island of the mind.

They seemed to be walking upward at a slight incline, and after about ten minutes' walk—the cost of excavating the tunnel must have been enormous, even in a part of the world where mining was almost as much a natural human activity as talking or sleeping or breathing—the path began to level out.

They came to a door of brushed steel or something similar, with an artificially lit combination lock of a type that Sophie had never seen before. She edged toward it to see if she could get a closer look, but though it was really just pure disinterested curiosity, it made the gatekeeper shove her away and utter a cloud of reproachful words, standing between Sophie and the matrix of the lock so that Sophie couldn't at all see what she was doing, let alone what numbers she pressed.

The door swung open, and Sophie moved through the portal and found herself in the most amazing room she had ever seen. It was a glorious high atrium, like the nave of a cathedral, and everything—walls, floors, what little furniture there was—was made entirely of ice.

"What on earth . . . ?" Sophie said to herself. To be alone in this enormous place . . . She felt like the last person alive.

"Amazing, isn't it?"

The voice came from behind her.

At the far end of the room, a white column of a figure had appeared and was gliding toward Sophie. It was the Snow Queen, Elsa Blix herself, dressed in a sort of mantle of white fur and almost as beautiful as the gleaming ice around her, which was subtly lit with a blue and purple and pink radiance that reminded Sophie of the nighttime illuminations at the Tivoli Gardens.

"Things have worked out better than I hoped," said Elsa Blix, "and with a symmetry, even an inevitability, that I scarcely could have imagined."

"What do you mean?" Sophie asked, though she had an inkling.

"I took your friend Mikael in nothing more or less than a fit of pique," said Elsa Blix, sounding more meditative than Sophie had expected her to. "Little did I know that he would prove the perfect bait for the fish I really wanted to catch. . . ."

Sophie's heart began pounding, and she had to stop herself from turning and beginning to run. Suddenly she felt too cold and tired to be afraid. She was filled with the conviction that Mikael needed her *now,* not after a lot of palaver about Elsa Blix's elaborate schemes and weapons and peace and whatever it was about Sophie's personal history that had led to her getting caught up in this absurd narrative featuring world-historical players like Niels Bohr and Alfred Nobel and Elsa Blix herself.

"Where is Mikael," she said roundly, "and is he all right?"

"Your friend is in grand health," Elsa Blix said in that strange hoarse voice she had, "though you may find him a little colder than the last time you saw him—but he has come along very nicely, I think."

"Might I see him now?" Sophie asked.

"You shall see him but not speak with him," said Elsa Blix. "You and I have business to discuss before I will release him from his bonds."

The thought of Mikael in cuffs and chains filled Sophie

with horror. What if Elsa Blix changed her mind about letting them both go?

The Snow Queen showed no sign of moving, and Sophie said nervously, "Can we see him *now?*"

Elsa Blix laughed. She was an outrageously beautiful woman—every slight gesture or turn of the head was arresting, and her charms made Sophie want to hit her.

"The impatience of youth!" she said lightly, her words irksome in a way that paradoxically brought Sophie back to herself again. She could smell the wet wool of her jumper and feel the supreme itchiness of the skin on her calves, which over her weeks of northern travel had become dry and scaly to a potentially madness-inducing degree. She surreptitiously bent down and gave the left calf a good scratch through the layers of clothes, Trismegistus twining quietly through her ankles.

It occurred to her that the pads of his paws must be very cold, but she did not want to draw attention to him by gathering him up in her arms.

"Come," said Elsa Blix, holding out a hand to Sophie.

Sophie grimly kept her own hands at her side. She was not the hand-holding type, and of all people in the world the one she least wanted to hold hands with was Elsa Blix!

The ice maiden let her hand drop after a moment; she seemed untroubled by Sophie's rudeness, and Sophie thought again that one of the most sinister things about the woman was her ability to remain unruffled.

They left the great ice chamber through an arched doorway of sorts and began climbing an elegant curved staircase, its individual risers made from blocks of ice glimmering with color; the overall effect was highly disorienting because of the lack of windows, which meant that one could not tell whether one were above- or belowground, in a cave or a mountain aerie.

They passed along a corridor of ice—was the place built newly again every winter, Sophie suddenly wondered, or could it be maintained year-round?—and came to a chamber that seemed to be separated from the corridor only by a thin curtain of clear glass beads hanging on strings.

"Go ahead," said Elsa Blix as Sophie put forward a hand to push the strings apart and see what was on the other side. "Nothing will hurt you here."

With this encouragement, Sophie used both hands to pull apart the curtain of beads. There was no further physical barrier, and yet in every other respect, Sophie could not have been more certain that she was looking at a prison cell, and that the figure under the heap of furs on the bed in the corner—the bed, too, was made of ice!—was Mikael.

"Mikael!" she called out, falling to her knees beside his bed and putting her hands on his cheeks.

But he slumbered on, his chest rising and falling regularly, his face pale and his features more like marble than anything living.

"He can't hear you," said Elsa Blix.

"Have you drugged him?" Sophie asked, her heart pounding with outrage and worry.

"He has been given a mild sedative," Elsa Blix admitted. "Nothing serious—only what you might take yourself if you had trouble going to sleep."

"Why hasn't he escaped from this room, then?" Sophie asked. "Those beads can't be the only thing keeping him here!"

"You're not wrong, Sophie," Elsa Blix said in that hoarse, gentle, infuriating voice. "It happens that the gas he inhaled during the attack at Niels Bohr's party rendered him peculiarly susceptible to certain hypnotic techniques. Some people are far less vulnerable than others to the effects of that particular drug. You, for instance, do not seem to have suffered any ill effects, though I imagine you must have inhaled as much of it as Mikael did. To you, this curtain is nothing more or less than a wall of beads that can easily be brushed aside. But to Mikael, the fourth wall of this room is exactly like the other three: solid ice. No more would he imagine he could pass through it than you, Sophie, would think you could fly through the air under your own powers."

Sophie turned and stared at her.

"Did you set off that bomb at the Mansion of Honor?" she asked incredulously.

"I did not," said Elsa Blix, "but I designed the weapon's prototype, and sold it to the Germans, so I was not surprised when they used it as part of a preliminary preparation for the invasion."

Sophie pulled back the scratchy wool blanket covering Mikael's body and felt his hands; they were as cold as one might expect, and she began chafing them between her own hands to try to warm them up.

"Come, Sophie, you will have plenty of time with Mikael later," Elsa Blix said briskly. "For now, I need you to prepare yourself to hear things of which your knowledge at present, I suspect, remains quite partial and imperfect."

"Things to do with my parents?" Sophie asked, feeling treacherous for allowing her desire for more information about them and their fate to overwhelm her scruples about communicating so freely with the person who had kidnapped her dearest friend.

Elsa Blix smiled.

"Yes, Sophie," she said, "that and more—but we will have something to eat first, and a drink of cocoa—you would like that, wouldn't you?"

In fact, Sophie was hungry and cold enough that she would have welcomed even a hard heel of moldy, stale bread and a cup of hot boiling water, let alone a cup of delicious cocoa. The story of Persephone was strong in her mind, though. Persephone was trapped in Hades for six months of every year for her *whole life* because of her own failure to withstand temptation in the form of the six pomegranate seeds whose consumption tied her forever to her captor. A woman who had developed the chemical compound that had transformed Mikael was a woman from whom one should not even consider accepting refreshments!

"Nothing to eat or drink, thank you," she said now, shaking her head. "The full story, please!"

"The full story—ah, Sophie, you are an idealist after all, not the funny little pragmatist I was led to expect. Can there even be such a thing as the full story?"

"Who have you been talking to about me?" Sophie said suspiciously.

Elsa Blix laughed. It sounded like the ringing of a bell, and Sophie hated her more than ever.

The room they had now entered had a beautiful array of food spread out on a low round table set between two great chairs, to which Elsa Blix led them. The chairs, which almost deserved the name *thrones,* were made not from ice but from a fine-grained dense wood that felt as hard and cold as stone.

Sophie planted her hands firmly on the armrests so that she would not accidentally reach out and eat something absentmindedly. There were beautiful berries of kinds that Sophie didn't recognize, and biscuits that looked like a very delicate and delicious form of shortbread, and slabs of smoked fish and sliced cucumbers and rye bread covered with poppy seeds and a silver jug of cocoa next to a bowl of whipped cream with a pretty little silver spoon to serve it with. None of it had any smell, though, Sophie realized a moment later, and she hardened her mind and her stomach.

"You're sure you won't have anything to eat?" Elsa Blix asked.

She poured herself a cup of cocoa—the cups and saucers were made out of a delicate, almost translucent porcelain glazed with white-on-white snowflakes—and lavished a huge dollop of cream on it.

Sophie's stomach growled involuntarily, and the tiny twitch of a muscle in Elsa Blix's cheek made Sophie suspect that the Snow Queen found Sophie's stubbornness amusing. She hoped she would be able to get away from here before too much longer—she had some ship's biscuit and dried fruit in her pocket, but she was not sure how long it would hold her.

"No, thank you," she said politely.

Elsa Blix selected a chocolate from the tray of sweets on the table. It was decorated with a crystallized violet, and when she had taken a delicate nibble, it could be seen that the cream inside was a faint violet also, or perhaps it just reflected the light in the chamber.

"It is long since time for Alfred Nobel to have departed this world," she announced. "He knows it himself: he has been alive—if one can call it that—for over a hundred years, and he exists in a haze of guilt and self-reproach at the fact of his being temperamentally unable to cut the cords binding himself to life. But one thing must happen before he is ready to go. . . ."

"The device," Sophie said. "The weapon my father was working on producing—the one Nobel believed would be so powerful that it would put an end to war. The one for which you have the plans!"

"Events are proceeding so quickly just now," said Elsa Blix, "that your father's device may soon be superseded, at least if the work Bohr and his colleagues are now pursuing comes to fruition. But the plans themselves still have more than ordinary interest, especially insofar as they may speed up progress toward actually building a bomb, detonation mechanism and all."

"Nuclear fission?" Sophie asked.

"Is that what they have decided to call it?" Elsa Blix said with interest. "It has also been called splitting the atom."

She fell silent, and Sophie ventured the timid observation that she did not really understand why she was there.

"I know you do not," said Elsa Blix. "Where to start, though?"

"I want to know what happened at the factory when my parents died," Sophie said, a little more boldly.

"Ah, yes," said Elsa Blix, "well, you are certainly aware of the fundamental issues, Sophie. I am not sure how much you know already, but perhaps I will begin by telling you that you know far more than you think you do, but that there is also one very important thing you do not know."

"All right," Sophie said impatiently, "tell me what that thing is, then."

"That is exactly what I intend to do," said Elsa Blix. "Sophie, you believe that we are enemies, but I can assure you that we have more in common than not."

How could that be?

Elsa Blix stood up and began pacing.

"I have been following the revelations in the Scottish papers about your great-aunt—your grandmother, I should say."

"So you know about that," Sophie said wretchedly. Gosh, how Tabitha would have hated the thought of Sophie having this particular conversation with someone like Elsa Blix! "I have not seen a Scottish newspaper for over a month; did they get hold of the story about Tabitha's relationship with Alfred Nobel, and put it all out there for everyone to see?"

"They did," said Elsa Blix. "It is now widely known that she gave birth to Alan Hunter herself, that he was Alfred Nobel's child, and that you, Sophie, are the grandchild and sole living heir not just of Tabitha Hunter but of Alfred Nobel."

"He did not have any children from his marriage?" Sophie asked.

"No," Elsa Blix said, sounding pained. "It happens he did have one other child, also outside of wedlock, but the fact of that child's existence is not known to him."

"He had another child?" Sophie said, surprised.

"First, a confession. Sophie, as soon as I began looking into this business of Tabitha Hunter and IRYLNS, I learned about your own visit there this past summer. You made your way in by a subterfuge—you had an appointment with a doctor next door and concealed yourself about the premises and then climbed over the wall to get into IRYLNS through the garden."

"Yes, that is correct," Sophie said. "Why does it matter to you, though?"

"It occurred to me that I might well be very interested in what you had said to that doctor."

"To Mr. Braid?" Sophie asked.

"He is a neurohypnotist, Sophie; do you remember that he put you into a trance and asked you questions about what you remembered of the accident that killed your parents?"

"How do you know this?"

"I had one of my people infiltrate his office and recover the records of your visit. He asked you questions, and you wrote down your answers; my agent photographed the pages, and we have had them transcribed. Sophie, your penmanship leaves much to be desired!"

Sophie looked at her with outrage. To be criticized for messy handwriting by a woman presumably responsible for all sorts of atrocities! But curiosity got the better of her.

"So what did I say?" she asked.

"You provided a very full and clear account of the incident—your language was childish, perhaps because you were so young at the time of the explosion, but I must admit that my own puzzlement as to how you survived was relieved by these passages."

"You have to tell me!"

"I will tell you, though you will likely be very angry with me indeed once you learn how it all happened."

"Were you directly responsible for the explosion?" Sophie asked. She did not know whether she would receive a straight answer, but she felt she might as well come out with the question.

"Not directly," said Elsa Blix, "but indirectly, yes, and morally you would certainly say I caused it."

"Did you pay that laborer to set the bomb, and then arrange for him to be killed afterward?" Sophie asked, thinking of what Nobel had told her about the Russian man who had fallen into a quarry.

"I arranged for someone to blow the place up," Elsa Blix said—how could she admit it so calmly? "But it was not a Russian laborer, Sophie, and it was not a matter of paying a bribe."

"So? Who was it, then?"

"Your mother, Sophie, had been having great difficulty sleeping in the months after you were born. She had become virtually unable to rest, and I offered my talents as a hypnotist to see if I could help her with relaxation exercises."

"She let you hypnotize her?" Sophie said, bemused but getting a very bad feeling about where this might be going.

"We had sessions two or three times a week for that whole autumn," Elsa Blix said. "I would put her under, and then give her a set of instructions. I had known for some months that I would have to leave; Alan and I did not share the same notions as to what should be done with the weapon, and I had begun to find working for Nobel almost unbearably constraining."

"What did you do?" Sophie asked, working hard to keep her voice level and unemotional.

"I gave your mother, while she was under hypnosis, a

set of instructions that would be cued by the simplest set of words—all I had to do was put a telephone call through to her while she was on the spot at the factory, and say to her, 'The snow is falling heavily now, Rose,' and she would pass into the trance state. Once in that state, I could tell her exactly what I wanted her to do, and she would not question any part of my instructions. I telephoned that day, and she did just as I told her to—she went and found a stick of dynamite and set it up with a detonator and blew the place up."

Sophie stared. The woman must be a sociopath. How could she describe this to Sophie so calmly?

"Aren't you going to ask me how you survived, though, Sophie?" said Elsa Blix.

"I don't want to have anything to do with you!" Sophie said, feeling quite sick.

"You have no choice," said Elsa Blix, sounding faintly confused.

Sophie suddenly wondered whether the Snow Queen might not have much less firm a grip on reality than Sophie had previously supposed—one could become very odd, she guessed, living in this kind of isolation.

"Your mother saved you, Sophie. This is what you described to Braid; your conscious self seemed to have no memory of it, but to your second self it was as clear and vivid as if you had seen the incidents earlier that day on a newsreel at the cinema. You described to Braid your mother picking you up but not responding at all to your cries and actually throwing you out of a window, with more strength than you imagined possible—and even as you landed on the ground outside the window, the thump of a massive explosion could be heard behind you. You had traveled just far enough from the building that you were quite safe, with only a broken leg; one of the workers in the outer area of the factory came and carried you away before the flames could reach you. The power of the maternal instinct had defeated even the most modern and scientific form of brainwashing in the world."

"What am I supposed to say?" Sophie asked incredulously. "Do you think it is all right for me to stand here and talk to you, as if I might ever forgive you for what you've done?"

"I look on this story as cautionary," Elsa Blix said, ignoring Sophie's question. "I should have made sure you would die. I did not know it then, but I had a very good reason to want you off the face of the planet."

"Why did it matter to you whether I lived or died?"

"I did not know then that your father was Nobel's son," said Elsa Blix. "If I had, my animosity would have run even deeper than it did—for I, too, am the child of Alfred Nobel. . . ."

"You are not!" Sophie said, though the words were more

expressive of shock and surprise than of actual disbelief. She remembered Nobel's having mentioned his acquaintance with Elsa Blix's socialite mother. It was at least feasible, she supposed, to imagine a liaison leading to the production of a child.

"The only thing I want, Sophie, is for you to go back to Nobel—thus far he has refused to admit me to his presence—and tell him this. Tell him he had another child, and that he needs to write a place for me into his will. You and I are the two heirs of Alfred Nobel, Sophie; I will not harm you, but you must go and plead my case. I will come with you, and you will persuade him to see me—a father cannot deny his child, can he?"

It was the most extraordinary thing Sophie had ever heard, and yet in a strange way she could see the justice of it.

"Why didn't you tell him before now?" she asked.

"I did not know it when I met him all those years ago," said Elsa Blix. "My mother told me only on her deathbed, though the man I have always known as my father was very cold to me in a way that made me suspect something was amiss, and of course my mother committed many later infidelities. But, Sophie, I think you cannot imagine the depth of the rage I have felt for Alfred Nobel, ever since he turned on me those many years ago. He hired me, he made me think of him as a sort of mentor, and then when push came to shove he took Alan's side against mine."

"But it was a question about the weapon, wasn't it?" Sophie said. "Not a personal question at all, but a philosophical one?"

"Is there any difference between the two things?" Elsa Blix asked.

Suddenly Sophie saw Elsa Blix as another version of Tabitha Hunter, someone impossibly distorted by a set of abstract commitments that in certain respects might have been admirable ones but that led to a kind of separation from the rest of humanity—a separation that negated the real, ordinary connections between human beings in which the ethical life must surely reside. There was some of Tabitha in Sophie, too, and Sophie could even feel that she had some shred of similarity to Elsa Blix, who was her aunt—her half aunt?—after all. Some, but not much—one could choose what kind of a person one would become.

"Even if I tell him this and he believes it," Sophie said slowly, "and even if he says he will see you, Nobel might not want to write you into his will."

"It is enough if he sees me," said Elsa Blix. "I am guessing that in his heart of hearts he knows I am his natural successor. He is a merchant of death—I am just showing him the true face of the work he has been doing all these years. I do not in all honesty care about the money. I will continue to build my own company, if he does not choose to bestow a share of his wealth on me. I want the public recognition that I am his child; only then will I destroy the plans, and if he will not acknowledge me in public, then I will sell them to the European Federation."

"The plans are for a bomb so powerful it could destroy an entire city, just like that," Sophie said slowly. "A bomb so small I could probably carry it in one of the panniers of my bicycle! You do not really mean to hand such a thing over to the federation, do you?"

"Nobody knows what I will do," said Elsa Blix, "not even myself. But once such a bomb has been conceived, sooner or later it will be built, for better and for worse—that is the nature of the human animal."

Sophie thought she spoke truly.

"Is that really all?" she asked. "I promise to say all this to Nobel, say it in a serious way, and just like that you will let me and Mikael go?"

"That is all," said Elsa Blix. "So long as you agree to the condition, I will fly you south this very evening. There is one other thing, I think, that I must ask before we go to find your friend. Those plans—do you know how they came into my possession?"

"How?" asked Sophie.

"That was not a rhetorical question," said Elsa Blix,

looking rather puzzled. "I genuinely want to know—I thought you must have had something to do with it, Sophie, at least once I learned of your existence."

"What do you mean?"

"Around the same time those images appeared on that absurd old-fashioned hunk of machinery in Edinburgh—I was able to obtain them by having one of my agents photograph the document from Nobel's files—I, too, received a sort of visitation."

"What was it?" Sophie asked.

"I thought you might have some notion yourself. I had a dream, a dream in which I very clearly saw your mother. Rose—ah, she was the only agent I could use for the destruction of the factory; nobody else would have let me hypnotize him or her so willingly, but I was sorry she had to die!"

Sophie stared at Elsa Blix. The woman was an utter psychopath—did she think Sophie could just ignore this sort of statement?

"In this dream," Blix continued, "your mother gave me a strangely precise set of instructions. I felt like a madwoman for following them, and the story of my adventures along the way is another tale altogether, but when I woke up I found myself under an almost irresistible compulsion to do just as she had told me. I went to the Fabergé workshop in Saint Petersburg and found a little old craftsman who had been consulted as to the metalworking technology needed for the explosive chamber of your father's device. After some persuasion—don't worry, Sophie, there was no violence involved, and it was only a slight stretch of the truth to represent myself as an emissary of your mother—he gave me a safe-deposit key that Rose Hunter had left with him more than fifteen years ago. I went to a bank on the Nevsky Prospekt; I was led to an underground vault, and there in a small metal box were the plans. . . ."

"Had my mother put them there?"

"Yes. Alan thought it too dangerous to have a second set circulating, and fought to keep everything within the factory, but your mother worried that sabotage might destroy all of his work and wanted to have some way of reconstructing it in the event of its being lost."

"But why should my mother have appeared to you in a dream?" Sophie cried out. "I would think she'd have done anything to keep those plans away from you—she died at your hands!"

Elsa Blix looked at Sophie in a way that could almost have been described as sympathetic.

"What if she knew that the plans were needed?" Blix said. "What if she had gathered that war was coming, and that Frisch and Meitner were just coming toward the point where Alan's work would have been peculiarly useful to them? What if she hadn't agreed with her husband that the bomb shouldn't be used?"

"She wouldn't have wanted the Hanseatic League to fall to the European Federation!" Sophie protested.

"That is certainly true," said Elsa Blix, "but then, neither do I."

Sophie stared at her. "But you sold them the weapons they used for the invasion of Denmark!" she said.

Elsa Blix shrugged.

"I am a weapons dealer," she said. "I sell to either side. I sell to anyone who has the money, within reason. That is the way of the world, Sophie, but no more than you would I like to see the world completely overwhelmed by Europe. It is sheer utopianism, though, to believe that one can prevent the most powerful weapon in the world from being built—your father was a utopian of that sort, but I was not, and neither was your mother. Indeed, even your precious Niels Bohr, Sophie, knows the weapon must be built—I have talked to him about it already. . . ."

"Are you really saying that you believe you were directed to the plans by my mother's ghost?" Sophie asked.

"That is indeed what I believe," said Elsa Blix.

Could it be that Sophie's mother had communicated with Sophie, too, without her even knowing it, but that the only message she had bothered to send had been a page of old blueprints? Sophie felt as though her brain had been twisted into knots. In a storybook, she would be plotting to kill Elsa Blix in revenge for her parents' death. In the real world, how would one even undertake such a thing? And what good could it possibly do?

"Come," said Elsa Blix. "We will have more time to discuss these matters later. You and I and Mikael will travel south in my aeroplane to see Nobel again so that we can hammer out the details of an agreement. It is time now for you to call Mikael back from his captivity."

"Are the changes in him permanent?" Sophie asked. If Mikael's former self were beyond reclamation . . .

"Time is the chief antidote," said Elsa Blix, which did not seem to answer the question. "Would you like to see Mikael now? And perhaps you will first use the washroom."

Sophie flushed. Her face *was* quite dirty, she knew it, and her hands were filthy, and she would welcome the chance to use the washroom—but why should this woman, herself surely almost beneath contempt morally, so readily induce in Sophie shame for what was, after all, merely physical dirtiness?

They seemed to be the only warm, living physical beings in the entire palace. The gatekeeper had not reappeared since Sophie had emerged from the tunnel, and Elsa Blix herself showed Sophie to a small washroom. The facility was a perfectly ordinary-looking porcelain one, to Sophie's relief. She did not want to have to set her bottom on a rim of ice!

"Now you may see Mikael," the Snow Queen told her, and they made their way through chambers and passageways built on a more than human scale to the strange cell where Mikael was being kept.

He was awake this time. He sat listlessly at the edge of the bed, elbows on his knees, face in his hands. As they watched, he looked up, then got up and began pacing around his cell. Something caught his attention in the corner, and he knelt down and began fiddling with what seemed to be a kind of jigsaw puzzle, only made of flat, irregularly shaped pieces of ice.

"Go and help him with the puzzle," Elsa Blix said, standing with her arms folded by the bead curtain.

"Mikael," Sophie said softly, reluctant to cross the threshold. She felt strangely self-conscious—was it because he was a captive and she was free, or because she had been watching him already without his knowing it?

He lifted his head up and turned it toward her, then went back to what he was doing, trying and failing to press another piece of ice into the edges of the one already set into the floor.

"He sees you," Elsa Blix whispered, "but he does not believe that you are really here. He thinks you must be merely another illusion. Go to him, Sophie!"

The thought that Blix might want to trap her with Mikael in the cell had already crossed Sophie's mind, but she had come so far, and had already so thoroughly given herself into Blix's power, there was no point hanging back now.

"Mikael, it's me," she said more loudly, stepping across the lintel and walking toward him. "I am really here. . . ."

"Sophie?" he said, looking up from the strange shards of ice before him and frowning. "But how can you be Sophie? How did you get here?"

As she looked at him, tears began to form at the edges of her eyes. She impatiently ran a finger along her lower eyelid and forced herself to think of non-sad things: earwax, pork sausages, the taste of anise.

Mikael was pallid, chilly, otherworldly.

He looked in her direction again, frowning a little.

Sophie was almost sure it was just wishful thinking—how could one tell such a thing just by looking at someone?—but had he not lost some of the hardness about the face that had been so striking during their days in Stockholm?

Trismegistus had followed Sophie over the threshold into the cell and was inspecting Mikael's ice puzzle with interest. He gave a little chirp and sniffed one of the pieces, then lapped at it a few times with his pink tongue.

"I don't understand how you came to be here, Sophie,"

Mikael said, his voice stronger now.

"It took me many days of travel," she said softly, and then, irrepressibly: "I was traveling by reindeer!"

"Reindeer?" Mikael said, his voice sounding a little more animated.

"Reindeer!" Sophie said. "And Trismegistus came with me—I must say that he has been very good—but, Mikael, I had to leave the bicycle in Stockholm. . . ."

"Sophie?"

"What?"

"Are we going to be able to leave this place?"

Sophie looked over at Elsa Blix, who was standing just to one side of the doorway, her hands crossed over her chest, the language of her body taut and defensive.

"I think so," Sophie said. "But, Mikael, it is good to see you!"

Tris was poking one of the puzzle pieces with his paw. He meowed to attract Sophie's attention, and she turned her gaze to what he was looking at.

She saw at once how the remaining pieces should fit together, and she bent down to rearrange them. As she fit the last piece into place, she heard a kind of click, and the whole puzzle began to rotate on its base.

Tris jumped back from it, the dainty haste of his steps almost comical, but Sophie could now see that the image chiseled in sharp lines on the surface of the puzzle was the chemical structure of nitroglycerin, traced over with a pattern she didn't recognize of interlocked elliptical orbits.

"Sophie!" Mikael said, turning to her and placing his hand on her sleeve. "I was so awful to you those last days in Sweden—how will you ever forgive me?"

Sophie found herself in his arms, her face muffled against the rough cloth of his jacket.

She wrapped her own arms around him.

"Sophie!" he said, his lips brushing her hair, his arms closing more tightly around her.

"The thing is," she said, though she spoke the words into his shoulder and she was almost certain he couldn't hear them, "it is *perverse* to have these tales of rescue and self-sacrifice and redemption of the other. In real life, when someone has been utterly horrible, there is every reason to think that they will continue to be so. It would be more productive and less self-defeating to write that person off and turn over to a fresh page. . . ."

She felt his hand brush her hair again, and buried her face in the hollow near his collarbone.

She saw suddenly that the war had changed everything and it had changed nothing. Perhaps Sophie would return to Scotland for university; perhaps she would instead get caught up in the war effort somewhere and become a cryptographer or an air-traffic controller or an ambulance driver. The legacy of her parents, their complex entanglement with the life and fortunes of Alfred Nobel, did not have to continue to define her. She was not obliged to be Sophie the student, Sophie the orphan, Sophie the worrier. She was just Sophie Hunter, with all sorts of adventures still to come.

"What are we going to do now?" Mikael said into her ear.

"We are going home," Sophie answered, knowing that it did not matter whether they ended up in Stockholm or Edinburgh or anywhere else, so long as Mikael was always with her.

AUTHOR'S NOTE

As I wrote in the note printed at the end of *The Explosionist,* which tells the earlier part of Sophie's story, I have always been in love with the idea of north. My father is Scottish, and I spent quite a bit of time in Edinburgh and its environs as a child. Over the summers between 2000 and 2004, I was lucky enough to visit St. Petersburg in Russia, Tallinn in Estonia, Stockholm in Sweden, and Copenhagen in Denmark. (København is the Danish spelling, which I have retained here for the slight sense of alienation and estrangement it gives to English-language readers.)

Like Edinburgh, these are cities of striking natural and artificial beauty, and I began to dream about what it would be like to live in an alternate universe in which these northern cities, so strongly united by culture and geography, were also politically connected. What if a new Hanseatic League (the Hanse was the name for the medieval trade alliance that spanned the Baltic and North seas) had come about in the wake of an event that did not happen in our world, but did take place in Sophie's—Napoleon's defeat of Wellington at the Battle of Waterloo on June 18, 1815?

There is a by now well-established genre of fiction called alternate history. Many alternate histories take a single event (often a famous battle) and change its outcome, considering what might have happened had history continued along another prong of the fork in the road. Novels of this sort might be set in worlds where the South won the American Civil War or Germany won World War II, to take two of the most popular examples.

Sophie is coming of age in a 1930s that looks in many respects much like the decade we knew (more about this in a moment), but that is in other respects quite different. As in our world, the 1910s in Sophie's world saw a Great War; in Sophie's world, though, that war lingered well into the 1920s and ended with England falling to Europe. The countries in the Hanseatic League (chiefly Scotland, the Netherlands, Denmark, Norway, and Estonia) are able to hold out against the Europeans only because they are also the world's premier suppliers of top-quality munitions, which Europe needs. Thus the secular patron saint of the modern Hanseatic states is Alfred Nobel, the Swedish chemist and industrialist whose invention of dynamite in 1867 changed the landscape of Sophie's Europe even more decisively than our own.

The world I imagined comes out of real places and real history but also out of fairy tales and counterfactual paths not taken. Of course, if we really think about how history works, a world that split off more than a hundred years prior to the events of *Invisible Things* would have much less in common with our own world. In Sophie's world, it is Ludwig Wittgenstein (in real history, a philosopher rather than a physicist), not Werner Heisenberg, who collaborates with Niels Bohr and comes upon the notion of the uncertainty principle; in our world, Denmark was occupied by the Germans in April 1940, whereas the world of *Invisible Things* sees a German-dominated European Federation invading Denmark in October 1938. But Sophie's world remains quite recognizably entwined or entangled with our own world and its history; not just Niels Bohr but Paul Dirac, Wolfgang Pauli, Otto Robert Frisch, Lise Meitner, and others were real historical characters with the same names and birth dates and personal histories that they possess in *Invisible Things*. Logically speaking, it is monumentally unlikely that if history had taken such a different turn there would even be such a person as Niels Bohr: he would have to have been the product of a particular meeting of sperm and egg contributed by parents who might never even have existed in the world of *Invisible Things*, let alone been born and met and married and conceived exactly the same child at the same exact moment and given him the same name as they did in ours. This is a very great liberty, given the rules of alternate history, and I have taken it ruthlessly and without remorse.

Particular thanks are due to Felicity Pors at the Niels Bohr Archive, who told me the story of Hevesy's cats that prompted me to get hold of Hevesy's delightfully titled collection of scientific papers, *Adventures in Radioisotope Research*, and to the friends who made my northern travels so pleasurable, especially Troy Selvaratnam, Vijai Maheshwari, and Tarvo Varres. Brent Buckner hosted much of the writing, kept me more or less sane in times of adversity, and gave useful comments on several rounds of draft. My father, Ian Davidson, offered scientific fact-checking at various stages. The book benefited immeasurably from editorial comments from Zareen Jaffery and Ruth Katcher. Thanks, too, to Kathleen Anderson, Liz Gately, and others at Anderson Literary Management. So many friends, family members, and students facilitated the writing of the book in one way or another that I really cannot begin to list them here, but I am immensely grateful for their contributions, and for the work of everyone at HarperTeen. Finally, I would like to thank the bloggers who greeted *The Explosionist* with such enthusiasm and asked for the sequel. I hope *Invisible Things* will meet or exceed their expectations.

The original inspiration for this story was Hans Christian Andersen's "The Snow-Queen," a tale I have loved ever since I first encountered it as a small child reading Andrew Lang's *The Pink Fairy Book*. Go and read it if you have not already!